WELCOME TO THE

WYRD
WEST

GO BEYOND LEGEND

LEGENDS OF THE WYRD WEST

GHOST RIDERS

Bound by the spectres of an old frontier myth, a posse must defy the forces of the Law to do what is right and go beyond legend.

BROKEN WINGS

Erica's father suffers a manic fever to build a Flying Machine, but refuses to believe that a terrifying monster lurks below their ranch.

DREAD RECKONING

Royce Falco faces his last midnight in the haunted Hayworth Penitentiary before being sent to the gallows the next morning.

HORSE NATION

The Tobin brothers, investigating unexplained phenomena, become part of an Indian ceremony that they didn't know they were destined to join.

SILENT ECHOES

The only evidence of people vanishing from Echo Station are the telegraphed messages wired to Sundown, telling of sinister plague doctors.

WYRD WEST

GHOST RIDERS

L.T. PHOENIX

Ghost Riders

Copyright © L.T. Phoenix 2020

Published by Phoenix Forge.

Print: ISBN: 9780994642615
Digital ISBN: 9780994642608

5.2

GHOST RIDERS

"Beyond the years of their Civil War, the forces of lawful American society pushed further into the untamed Wild West. During this time of upheaval arose a posse of unlikely outlaws, their Fate bound to an old frontier legend…"

– Charles Lafayette

PROLOGUE

FALL FROM GRACE

Jacobi heard them again, as though lost voices trailed on a wind accompanied by a rhythmic beat, like a faint chorus from Beyond.

"Jacobi?" came a piercing interruption. "Another beer?" That irritating voice though, could find him even in other rooms, cutting through the strange haze of voices and sounds that he was trying to focus upon over the normal hum. Jacobi's face fell into his hands at the poker table, releasing a sigh of frustration. Francis was calling for him out of earshot, again, even though the poker room they were playing in was around the corner from the bar.

Francis and Jacobi were on board the *River Grace,* a luxurious paddle steamer that promised the thrill of high-stakes gambling while taking in the frontier sights of the Rubicon River. The steamer departed the modern city of La Grande on the river's east side, climbing the map northward, destined to find port in the logging town Rosewood on the river's west side after a few days travel.

Somewhere along the way, Francis had landed them in danger.

Seated across the poker table from Jacobi was Charles Lafayette, twizzling his curling moustache, a mysterious man whose verbose claims included him to be a famous magician. Unlike most others, he didn't remove his hat indoors, and it was as though the overly-wide midnight blue brim created more of a shadow upon his face than it should have.

Each time the magician's piercing azure gaze stared upon him through that veil of shadow, Jacobi caught sound of those distant voices again, wailing from beyond the confines of the steamer. He dared not ask anyone if they heard the inexplicable noises as it seemed apparent that they did not, and Jacobi did his best not to appear peculiar as the magician watched him look for the wailing.

On the other side of the dealer to the magician, smoking a fat cigar, was the owner of the Matthias Mining Consortium, or "M.M.C." as she often stated with bold pride.

Twyla Matthias' sinister boasting, endless supplies of money and the pair of uniformed U.S.

Army guards holding rifles nearby, all cast her as an extremely dangerous woman.

Upon Francis' meandering return with two bottles of beer in hand, those at the table were interested in the Boston gentleman's answer to where he was going to get the money owed to Ms Matthias. Money that he said he and Jacobi would "be good for."

Twyla Matthias closed her bejewelled gold pocket watch, not so much because she had been looking at the time on one side or using the mirror to check her flawless skin on the other, but more to flaunt her excessive wealth.

"Francis and Jacobi from Boston, Massachusetts..." She spoke deliberately, annunciating disbelief in Francis' previous tales by pushing the last syllables of their names and place of origin so hard it almost sounded like hissing. "Two dandy Boston boys travel westward and find fortune along the way in Boom Town, prospecting claims enough to buy ranches and cattle, suddenly wealthy cowboys... But they do not have enough on hand to pay their way out of a bad hand of poker, not even some gold from your fortuitous prospecting?" Twyla pushed her gold-rimmed spectacles closer to her face, Francis and Jacobi seeing their worrisome reflections in them. "I happen to know a thing or two about gold mining, and I've never heard of you two, but the *River Grace's* register has you listed as one Francis Geddes and one Jacobi Nicholson, from Boston, Massachusetts. Two dandy boys from Boston, that I assume have never travelled west enough to have ever reached Boom Town, and that now owe me five hundred and seventy-nine dollars and fifty-five cents..."

"Well, we, uh," Francis spilled beer on his floral-patterned vest as he put the other bottle down on the table with a drunk hand next to his friend. Getting back into his chair with clumsy poise, Francis then knocked that bottle and the bowl of nuts beside it into Jacobi's lap, "we uh..."

"Frank!" Jacobi stood up, trying to wipe away some of the dampness. "Excuse us a moment, *Gentleman, Lady*. I need to have a serious talk to my *friend*." He grabbed Francis by the shoulder, "Come on," leading him.

Twyla waved for her blue-uniformed guards to let them go. "They'll be back, won't you boys? Besides, we're surrounded by a whole lot of river with nowhere else to go..."

Jacobi snatched their boater hats from the hooks near the door, guiding his stumbling *friend* outside into the night.

Grasping a railing with white knuckles at the edge of the paddle steamer, too mad to take in the splendour of the starlit American Frontier across the river's edge, Jacobi turned on Francis. "You always do this, Frank. You never shut up. And you land us in the most ridiculous situations. I can't stand it!" Jacobi was livid. After years of Francis getting on his nerves, he was ready to break. "We owe over five hundred dollars because you're an idiot and don't stop!"

Francis took a sip of what was left of his beer, attempting to think. He then pushed Jacobi. "I don't like the way you're talking to me."

"Well, I don't like talking to you at all," Jacobi pushed him back, "and I just wish you would just shut up for just five minutes!"

Francis managed to slap the boater hat off Jacobi's head, the hat spinning overboard.

"Fugg you, Frank!" Jacobi took both sides of Francis' own boater hat, lifted it off his head and then pulled it down so hard that his head popped through the inner brim. "You've had that coming for years!"

Francis made a wild swing with his beer bottle across Jacobi's face, liquor and shattering glass falling about the deck.

There was no way that Jacobi was going to be able to return the gesture as his world turned upside-down, spinning, blood flowing from a gash across his face. As he tried to hold onto the rail and consciousness, he could hear the voices again, almost singing, alongside an approaching rumble.

In his drunken stupor, Francis didn't realise the extent of the blow to his friend's face as he lifted Jacobi's legs and began hoisting him over the guard rail. "Perhaps a splash in the river will sorry you up."

As the *River Grace's* security approached too late, followed by Twyla Matthias and her army guards, Francis passed out from excessive inebriation.

Loose from Francis' limp grip, Jacobi Nicholson fell overboard while hearing a beating rhythm like thundering hooves accompanied by a wailing chorus of voices. In his delirium, as he fell from the *River Grace* toward the depths of the Rubicon River, Jacobi caught sight of ghostly riders upon horses flying through the starlit night sky.

PART I

GOING WEST

CHAPTER 1

The monstrous beast had snapped its wide jaws around the bloodied Jacobi. In a moment of predacious opportunity, it had claimed its prey and wrenched him through the waters of Rubicon River. Blood continued to flow from his face as each attempted stroke of escape was exchanged for a mouth-full of river water.

Questions fought their way through Jacobi's excruciating delirium. Had he truly seen the ghostly riders that belonged to the mysterious sounds he had been hearing all night, or were they a figment from the blow to his head? Whatever they were, they must have been left behind.

There were faint beacons of hope in the distance of Rubicon River. Could some of those lights be the *River Grace* he'd fallen from? Or perhaps they shone from La Grande where the steamer had departed. He couldn't know. The monster had wrestled and rolled him through the water far from the paddle steamer.

Of all the lights that could be seen, to him, it wasn't the starlit night that shone brightest of all against the slicked black scales of the beast, it was the creature's eyes glowing a scarlet red like the embers of a dying fire.

With crushing teeth, the dark alligator-like monster swam with the screaming Jacobi in its jaws far from the *River Grace*, like some water dragon from fables he'd read. Surely, he'd die. With each spluttered breath of more-water-than-air, this would be his end. Darkness overtook him every few moments, then waking, then fading to black again.

The dragon reached a shore. The spectral riders had returned - cowboys on flaming horses materialising in from the night air, circling above the monster as though it was carrion. Amidst them was a barbarian of dark fire with feathers in his wild hair riding a great bird that thundered and released sparks of lightning with each beat of its mighty wings among the horse's resounding hooves and their rider's sombre dirges.

Upon the winged storm, the savage drew a bow formed of antlers and pulled back on an arrow, aiming at the wingless dragon. The armoured beast shook its prey, unrelenting, when the arrow bounced from its pitch hide.

The other spectres rode through the air with the feathered-one as though there were stable ground beneath the burning hooves of their phantom steeds. They fired revolvers with bullets of hellfire and threw lasso loops of burning steel at the monster.

The savage drew another arrow from nothingness, pulling back upon a bow string formed of wind, releasing it as a stroke of lightning toward the monstrous dragon.

Jacobi heard the frightful riders singing a terrifying tune during a waking moment, so very reminiscent of the distant voices he couldn't place earlier, but to his ears now sounded with the clarity of an unwanted requiem.

The dragon wouldn't give up its dying prize, but neither would the ghostly riders in the sky.

Another arrow of lightning finally released Jacobi from the black dragon's maw, striking the beast in one of its crimson eyes. The monster scurried into the trees of a river foreshore under the starry night followed by its ghostly hunters.

When Jacobi regained consciousness, the sun was shining bright and the world appeared to be moving away from him. He was rested upon some form of stretcher bed that was supported by two long poles that dragged their ends in the earth. Something was pulling the contraption, so it was actually he that moved away from the world that he could see.

Jacobi tried to look around.

His body was wrapped in various bloodied rags. Although he was fastened to this makeshift moving stretcher, he wasn't tied down as such that he thought he was somebody's prisoner.

Almost as if to answer his confusion, a dog with a thick fur coat slowed its walk to then match pace with the moving stretcher. Jacobi's heartbeat had skipped when he thought - for a split-second - that it was a wolf, but this was simply a dog with volumes of red and white fur. It pulled along its own angled stretcher, similar, but much smaller, to the contraption Jacobi rested upon.

The dog was, thankfully, cheerful, tongue panting slightly and tail wagging. It studied him with curiosity from eyes of two different colours: the left blue and the right brown. Jacobi swore the dog was trying to smile at him as it pulled its own load of trappings along the same worn dirt path as whoever or whatever was dragging him.

Jacobi wrestled with the bindings that kept him from falling out of this angled bed, loosening them enough to look around.

He was in agony. He touched his face to a stinging response, pressing upon some sort of fixing on the bottle wounds. He had wrapped injuries from the monster's teeth - had it actually been some sort of dragon? - along his ribs and limbs, and he wasn't exactly travelling in any form of luxury that would help his predicament. Although laying down, his patched head was high enough, that even in his groggy state, he could see down his bandaged and padded body to his shoeless feet and the trail left behind that had led through a forested area.

Jacobi could hear a chant in a language that he didn't recognise. Thankfully, it was nothing like the chorus of death he had recently experienced.

He forced his neck to turn against protesting muscles and wound dressings, seeing that a reddish-brown horse with fur saddlebags was dragging his stretcher.

The horse's rider looked back to face Jacobi. Rumpled hat with feather, long dark hair underneath also decorated with a feather, a face like... dark fire.

It was the savage - an Indian! - from when he passed out in that monster's jaws. But, did all that really happen, with the ghostly riders, the thundering bird, and the black dragon? What were all those terrifying visions he saw when he went overboard and was almost dragged to his death?

It could have been a nightmare, but the all-too-real wounds would certainly disagree. But, now the barbarian was riding a horse and wearing clothes no different to any other person he'd seen while travelling closer to the West with Francis.

And... where was Francis?

Jacobi winced, his head throbbing.

The Indian met Jacobi's gaze with a smile, nodded, and tipped his hat with a salute of two fingers from the brim. "Welcome back..."

Perhaps not, Jacobi thought, overwhelmed with pain and confusion as his world faded to black again.

CHAPTER 2

The appetising aroma from a small pot hanging over a crackling campfire woke Jacobi from his wounded slumber. The smell wasn't like anything he'd ever experienced before.

"Would you like some coffee?" The voice was strong, but gentle. The same voice that had been chanting a foreign song.

The Bostonian startled. Jacobi didn't realise that the barbarian from his overboard nightmare, the Indian that seemingly rescued him, was just nearby preparing something from a metal pot above a fire.

"It, uh..." Jacobi was hesitant, "doesn't smell like coffee." He was unsure how safe he was around a savage of the Wild West. Travelling with Francis, they had heard terrible tales of Indians robbing wagon caravans, stealing horses and scalping settlers.

The Indian smiled, almost chuckling. He wasn't covered in warpaint or an abundance of feathers and beads as the stories had told. "This may be the best coffee you have ever had." He came over, handing a metal mug to Jacobi, long dark hair falling about a leather vest.

The dog was there, following with great interest as it watched the mug exchange from tan fingers to pale hand. Ever present, the red dog that could be mistaken for a wolf, circled around until it found sniffing Jacobi and his medical coverings more exciting. He couldn't see the Indian's horse, but the saddle and baggage were nearby.

The Indian returned to an area of gathered firewood. He resumed fashioning something of branches, twine and fur.

Jacobi tasted the coffee. "This is nothing like Boston coffee!" A wondrous sensation filled him as the hot liquid slid over his tongue and down his throat, as though half his wounds gave up complaining in exchange for the pleasurable liquid filling his body. "Amazing... What's your secret?"

"Eggshells," the answer was delivered with a wry smile, "and *Indian* magic..."

Jacobi's wounded muscles twinged across his back, but to a lesser degree. "Pardon my asking, but I'm guessing that's not a wolf?" He hoped he was asking the right questions as he still didn't know how safe he was, whether he was a prisoner or not.

"Buddy?" The Indian shook his head. "He's only a wolf in *spirit*," he answered, tapping his chest with a gentle fist. We do not... my people, we do not make much of a distinction. He's not a wolf as you may understand it. Breeders of the lands far north call his kin, *husky*. Some call him *dog*, while the few that know him call him *Buddy*."

Jacobi ran some undamaged fingers through the thick red and white fur upon the agreeable animal. "*Buddy*... was it an obvious choice of name?"

The Indian became lost in thought for a moment, recalling his oldest memory of the dog. "*Buddy* was the only name he would respond to."

"He's very friendly."

"He doesn't usually accept strangers so quickly – he must see a kindness in your spirit." The Indian looked fondly at the happy dog. "Those that cross him... well, I have seen men in worse situations in Buddy's teeth than when you were in that monster's jaws."

"Speaking of that..." Jacobi wanted to know more. The Indian mentioning the creature brought the memories to a fuller state of factuality, a place in his mind where he could accept that the events after falling overboard really did occur. "What was that thing?"

"For generations, the people of Mudflats have called it a *Terror Gator.*"

"Is it some type of alligator?"

"Perhaps, but that all depends on your perception. It's not like any normal alligator. There are stories told, most of it forgotten over the years or remembered as myth. But as you know it, it is as surely real as you and I speaking to each other about it now. There are many mysteries in these lands, *Stranger*, and not everyone can see them... or chooses to see them."

Jacobi thought that the Indian's grasp of the English language was excellent; it wasn't the broken American English he'd been told that only a scant few could manage. "Speaking of seeing things, I can't even believe what I'm about to say, so pardon me when I ask... Who... or what... were those men that rode through the sky?"

"Men?" The Indian stopped his crafting.

"Those men that rode through the sky on horses around you, while you rode on a gigantic storming bird, all of you riding after me and the monster..."

"There were no others; I was alone on my horse."

"Fugg me!" Jacobi pressed the dressing on his face. "Excuse my cussing, but I really must have been out of sorts."

"I rode after the Terror Gator, my arrows not piercing its hide. I was trying to convince it to drop you and scurry back to its lair. It would have smashed your bones and buried you alive until you were soft and bloated enough to chew, or perhaps delivered you to a fate far worse than that."

"What's worse than that?" Jacobi's skin went impossibly paler. "It was good luck that you were there!"

The Indian had become pensive after learning of the invisible riders. "Luck played no part, but *Fate* was with you that night."

"Aren't they the same thing?"

"That's another matter that depends on your perception."

Jacobi was becoming confused. "So, not luck but *Fate* - why do you say that?"

"I have been tracking a cruel woman, Twyla Matthias, for many winters now." The Indian returned to his crafting. "She was on your boat."

"Twyla Matthias! She's why I fell overboard. Francis, the idiot I was travelling with, managed to get us into debt for over five hundred dollars to her. Francis and I had a fight over it, and, as you know, I didn't come out of it so well."

"It was Buddy that alerted me to your struggle far from the paddle steamer and its people looking for you overboard. He sensed the Terror Gator with you in its jaws. So, we rushed to rescue you from the Rubicon River, riding alongside the water loosing arrows at the monster."

"That's when those devilish riders were there in the sky going after the monster with you, and you shot it in the eye with an arrow while they fired their flaming guns and threw hot ropes."

"I was definitely alone, there were no other riders."

Jacobi had become so sure of what he saw each time he spoke of it. "I'm telling you; they were cowboys from Hell, on flying flaming steeds... and they had faces like death... and you were at their lead riding a great bird and shooting lightning... Fugg! I can't believe what I'm saying, but I know what I saw."

The Indian didn't respond for a moment after that. Jacobi had never seen a man go so deep into thought before.

"So, who are you," the Indian asked, "he who sees ghostly riders and thundering birds?"

"My name is Jacobi..."

"Only Jacobi? The white men usually carry more names than that."

"Jacobi Nicholson... from Boston, Massachusetts."

The Indian came over to Jacobi and pulled excess blankets from him. "If you feel you are a prisoner, Jacobi Nicholson from Boston Massachusetts, you are not. You are free; we are always free."

Jacobi was relieved. "What do I call you?" He stood, not knowing how many days it had been since he had used his legs.

The Indian reached for his work, a crutch crafted from strong branches bound in entwined sinew and reeds with a fur support. As he placed it under Jacobi's armpit, he replied, "Which do you want to know? The name I was born with, the name I grew up with, the name the white men made me choose, the name I chose for myself...? There are many."

"That's a lot of names, but whichever one you like the most, the one you go by now." Jacobi thought a moment. "The name I would come to say to you as a friend, like I would say to Buddy."

The Indian smiled at the dog, reflecting. "Now you are making new friends for me?"

Buddy circled, tail wagging with a joyful response.

"In your tongue, people who come to know me, call me," – it seemed for a second that the Indian had to think about what his name was, as though he was about to speak one word but released another - "*Hawk.*"

"Like the bird?"

"With regard to saying it, yes."

"Thank you for helping me - for saving me!" Though it caused him pain, Jacobi extended a hand toward the Indian, "Thank you, *Hawk,* my new friend in the West."

Buddy interrupted with a gentle bark.

"Of course, you too, Buddy," Jacobi added.

Hawk stood there for a few seconds, staring at the gestured hand, then reluctantly took the handshake. "You are welcome, Jacobi Nicholson. Fate weaved this to be so."

Jacobi looked around at the camp. It appeared to be relatively packed away in wooden boxes, almost ready to move, with wrapped furs and skins piled on top. "Pardon me, Hawk, but are you able to tell me where I am to go from here?"

"One of the few white men I trust should be arriving today to pack the camp and take the goods I have crafted for sale. He will take you and teach you how to find your friend and find your way home."

"Oh, I'm done with Francis and Boston." Jacobi explained. "If *Fate* did play a part, as you say, in what's happened, then Fate did me a favour. I never have to see that idiot again - or go back East for that matter. As far as I'm concerned, I am free, as free as I have ever been. I'm going to make a new life here in the West; that's my Fate. The old me fell overboard from the *River Grace* and may as well have been eaten by that monster alligator in the Rubicon River. Rest in peace: Jacobi Nicholson, from Boston, Massachusetts."

There was something in the way Jacobi's mock-eulogy affected Hawk. "Take this," the Indian reached into his vest and pulled some sort of necklace with a charm from around his head, "keep it with you along your new journey."

"What is it?" Jacobi held the strange medallion of the necklace aloft by its leather strings, a long white feather hanging from it, studying the intricate wood carving:

Three evenly spaced vertical lines crossed through three evenly spaced horizontal lines, both sets of lines crossing through three evenly spaced concentric circles. The triple cross-upon-circle motif seemed to depict something between a snowflake and a spider's web.

"It is *Aetron.* That charm belonged to my brother, Royce, but he doesn't wear it and I don't need to hold onto it any longer," the Indian answered, revealing more of his self than he had in a very long time. "But, more importantly, one could ask, *what is it not,* for it is so many. You'll learn what it *is* as you and *Fate* decide it to be so."

"But, will your brother... Royce... miss it?"

Hawk answered that question by not answering it. "You are already spinning a new direction in your life, and I know, as a bird that beats its wings affects which wind we breathe, your Fate has already begun to weave into the lives of others."

A sharp gunshot rang out in the distance, bringing Jacobi's answers to an end. Black birds could be seen flying from trees. More shots were fired with the sound of galloping horses and wagon wheels following.

Bursting through brush into the campsite, a wagon drawn by two horses veered to miss the fire, but the vehicle drifted and smashed the hanging pot's hot contents over. The driver, a grey bearded man dressed in the rough fur and leather trappings of a frontier survivalist, brought the horses to a screaming halt, reloading his rifle. "Fugging Renegades on my tail!"

Hawk quickly grabbed his bow; the same antler bow Jacobi had seen in his vision while being torn to shreds by the Terror Gator. The Indian tossed him a revolver which he fumbled to catch, unfamiliar with handling weapons.

Two men in dishevelled grey military coats rode in upon horses, firing their revolvers. Hawk had already aimed and loosed an arrow into the intruder on the left, the grey coat falling to the earth with his horse fleeing the area. "Shoot the other one," Hawk commanded Jacobi, reaching for another arrow.

In a sheer panic, Jacobi held the gun toward the second man, eyes shut tight, squeezing the trigger as many times as he could, the exploding sounds and recoil forcing him to stumble back.

Of the six bullets Jacobi fired, one found its mark between the last man's eyes.

Jacobi fell to the ground, a ringing inside his head, stunned by the fact that he had just killed a man. Hawk lowered his next arrow, no longer needed, as the second horse bolted away.

"Fugginell." The bearded man laughed at Jacobi from the wagon, only just finishing reloading his last bullet. "Am I glad you're a lucky shot, Stranger!" His age was difficult to discern as he dropped down from the driver's seat, patting the wagon's two horses with thanks, calming them. Looking at the hole between his pursuer's eyes, he added, "I guess that could have been me!"

Jacobi dropped the revolver, a burnt smell filling his nostrils, his hands shaking with pain. He wasn't sure what was happening, if it was from the gun's recoil or the realisation of killing a man setting in.

"Howdy, Hawk," the new arrival greeted. He looked at the ruined campfire and the pot on its side, face screwing up with shame. "Well, I guess I missed the coffee?"

"My Friend." Hawk tapped his fist to his chest. "Our new Friend says it was *amazing.*"

"And who is this new… Friend?" the driver asked with casual calm as though being chased and fired upon were simply normal everyday fare. He noticed, in particular, the pendant hanging from the shaken stranger's chest.

"This is Jacobi," Hawk answered. "Can you take him with you and show him what life is really like here in the West?"

"Looks as though you've had a few good lessons already." He looked at the sorry young man that had been chewed up and spat out by the Wild West before even having properly set foot in it. "We'll have to teach you how to shoot, and I hope you can still work. The first lesson will probably be *how to dispose of dead bandits.*" The newcomer extended a gloved hand. "Howdy, the name's *Miller.*"

Jacobi accepted the hand, being pulled up to his feet, shaking it. "P-pleased to meet you, Miller. Um, my name is Jacobi Nicholson."

"Real proper, isn't he?" Miller looked to Hawk, smiling. "Shell-shocked, but still proper."

"And," Hawk added, "take him to see Charles Lafayette."

"Really?" Miller dropped the handshake, annoyance crossing his face.

Despite the sudden shift in greeting, Jacobi's eyes lit up with recognition of the strange magician's name from the *River Grace*. He still felt too shaken to interrupt in that moment, so let their conversation flow on to conclusion.

Miller asked Hawk, "It sounds like you're not coming, so where are you going?"

"To continue tracking Twyla Matthias." Hawk didn't let Miller respond, interrupting their exchange with a chirping whistle that Jacobi thought sounded exactly like a wild bird.

The horse that had dragged Jacobi's mortally wounded body by travois to the campsite trotted into the area, responding with a whinny to the Indian's whistled call. As Jacobi retrieved the revolver from the ground, he observed unusual horizontal dark stripes encircling the legs in the horse's golden-tan coat.

"If I find her," Hawk loaded his saddle with packed bags onto the horse, "I'm finally going to end it."

"That does worry me some." Miller's frown lines creased with concern, seeing the sincerity in Hawk's answer. "But tell me, why the fugg do we need to visit that dandy, Chuck Lafayette?"

"Because," as Hawk went from the camp, his answer left Miller speechless, "Jacobi Nicholson has seen the Ghost Riders."

CHAPTER 3

"The grey one on your left is *Sarge*," Miller explained, "and the dark brown one is *Maple Stirrup*."

Jacobi laughed. "*Maple Stirrup*, really?"

"Fugg yeah. Won him in card game from a Canadian."

"What was the one back at camp with the stripes called?"

"Hawk's horse? He calls that one, *Blaze*. Holds some significance to him. Anyways, stop changing the subject with horses." Miller wasn't putting up with it any longer.

"Jacobi is way too difficult. You could get shot in town just for having a name like that. *Jake* will do much better. I'm calling you Jake from now on. If you had been in the Service, I'd be calling you Nicholson – that's why everybody calls me Miller – but you ain't been in the Service."

"You were in the military?" Jacobi asked.

"I was," Miller sighed. "At first, conscripted into the war for the South. Later on, I got Sarge here."

"The Confederates?"

"The fugging Confederates." Miller shook his head. "I didn't like it, but that was where I lived, and I had to wear the same grey coat as those Renegades."

"Who were those men?"

"They call themselves *Renegades*." Miller thought how best to describe them. "They're an outlaw militia - worse, they're bandits – and they don't accept that they lost the war."

As the horse-drawn wagon rolled closer toward the settlement of Mudflats, the smoke from chimneys could be seen rising over the wet brown earth.

"Anyway, as I was saying before when I got tripped up on your name, *Jake*, I'm telling you: I was with Chuck Lafayette that night. He even made me go through a stupid summoning ritual to make him appear. There's no way he was on your boat during those days."

Jacobi didn't know what more to say. "I promise you, a man of that exact same name and description was at the poker table on the *River Grace...*"

Miller spat chewing tobacco over the side of the wagon. "I do actually believe you. Trust me, if you get to know Chuck, you'll be banging your head against a fugging brick wall with all the tricks and nonsense he pulls."

As Miller handled the reins, Jacobi realised there was a third on board. Buddy stood on hind legs amongst the crafted goods, front paws holding onto the edge of the wagon's wall, letting the warm morning breeze flow through his fur. "How long has the dog been with us?"

Miller looked back to the stowaway. "Not long. Happens all the time. He probably came back after us when he realised that he couldn't keep up with Hawk."

"Hawk abandoned his dog?"

"No, never." Miller put his eyes back on the damp trail. "Buddy doesn't really have a master. He has friends; he's an equal. He comes and goes as he pleases, but he rarely goes unless there's a problem. He's the messenger between friends that aren't always together, that keep on moving from place to place."

"Does he always find one of you?"

"Every time." Miller nodded with happy memories crossing his face. "He can go from settlement to settlement, hunt to feed and water himself, carry mail, drag part of a camp, and still find his way back to either of us." He turned to

Jacobi, "He can even help save a wayward Bostonian from the jaws of a Terror Gator."

The husky barked, leaping out of the wagon to the ground and took off ahead. Miller explained, "That means we must be close."

Around a minute later, Miller pulled alongside a crossroads of soaked earth at the outskirts of Mudflats, next to a large wagon that was practically a caravan. He helped the wounded Jacobi climb down from the wagon's seat, handing him the crutch Hawk had crafted.

Jacobi had seen some ostentatious displays travelling to the West, but this blue, red and black wagon was signed with gold lettering that read like the front of a cheap newspaper advertisement:

The One & Only
CHARLES LAFAYETTE
LEGENDARY MYSTERIOSO
Illusionist. Magician. Perceptivist.
Master of Cosmology,
Esoterica, Fortuna,
Portentia and Mysticism.

Miller admitted to Jacobi, "Thank fugg for that. He usually makes me do a song and dance to make him appear..."

Jacobi didn't understand what that meant.

There were no horses to be seen and no sign that anyone lived immediately nearby: just this unattended caravan with peeling paint on the side of the crossroad.

Buddy rushed up the few stairs at the back of the caravan and quickly disappeared inside through a hanging door that was just the right size for him, leaving it swinging within the bottom of an average-sized door.

Within seconds, something fell over inside the caravan, and a black cat bolted out of the little door, soon to be chased by the dog that had immediately gone looking for it.

"It's all right." A familiar voice opened the door, the occupant looking to Jacobi, "the animals are acquainted well."

Jacobi almost fell from his crutch: it was indeed the magician from the *River Grace.*

"Same man?" Miller asked.

"Same man," Jacobi confirmed.

The veteran shook his head with an irritated want to disbelieve.

"Do not be frightened," the magician spoke, "unless you were followed by a Terror Gator. You weren't followed by a Terror Gator, were you?"

"Uh," Jacobi's eyes searched the area, becoming worried, "no... could we have been?"

The caravan's occupant didn't answer as he came down the small set of stairs, smirking at the wounded Jacobi's worry. "Most excellent."

The man's midnight blue suit and wide-brimmed hat were as flamboyant as some of the gold lettering he pointed to. "These are freshly signed, Miller. What do you think?"

"You've changed some words?" Miller pointed at letters that weren't peeling like others.

"Indeed!" The magician looked to Jacobi. "Our Miller is still as canny as always. You see, M'laddo, *Occultist* and *Sorcerer* were not having the effect in civilised La Grande that I had hoped for. My assistant, she... resigned, and I was... asked... to leave."

"Ran out of town again?" Miller crossed his arms, smirking.

Lafayette nodded, admitting, "Well, it was an event, to be sure, but I wouldn't really call it an *attempted lynching*... this time..."

Miller shook his head. "So how many times is that now? Just don't get into trouble in Mudflats, Chuck, I need you to have a chat with Jake here."

"Dear Alfred," - that was the first time Jacobi heard Miller's given name - "you know it pains me so when you reduce my moniker to *Chuck* as though you're some common barroom brute. Despite the slight toward me, I will certainly converse with young... *Jacobi*

Nicholson, is it not, we met above water on the *River Grace?*"

The man tipped the wide brim of his hat toward Jacobi, acknowledging that they had met without being asked.

"Where are my manners? I'm positively aghast with embarrassment." He extended a white-gloved hand to Jacobi. "As you know, I am the One and Only, Charles Lafayette, Legendary Mysterioso... But, if it suits you, I will gladly accept *Magician.*"

Jacobi bit his lip softly, "Ah, yes, we've already met..."

"Of course, M'laddo," Charles Lafayette twizzled his dark moustache. "But never stop a magician when he takes a chance to practice his performance."

Miller rolled his eyes. "Hawk sent me with Jake to..." He grunted. "Apparently you already met Jake on a steamboat when you and I were actually somewhere else."

"Indeed," the magician answered.

"I assume you're not going to explain how you were in two places at once?"

"But, was I?"

"Fuggsake," Miller cussed, looking at Jacobi. "This is what Chuck does. Get used to it."

Miller continued, "Anyway, Jake saw something you'd know about."

Charles raised an arm to the entryway of his caravan. "Come, M'laddo, let me assist you up these stairs. We must discuss the nature of why you are here. I'm sure you have many questions."

Miller headed back to the wagon of crafted goods. "Hawk has gone tracking Twyla Matthias again," he looked at Lafayette with great sincerity, "apparently to finally end it. Last I heard, she was flashing her gold in Sundown. I don't know if Captain Cordell is with her, though I've heard he's been running sorties near Sundown. Anyway, I'll leave you two to get to know each other while I go into Mudflats to sell this load."

Climbing on board, Miller took the reins, starting the horses on their way. "Thanks, Chuck. And, Jake, for you, the Wild West is about to get a whole lot weirder!"

"How did you fit all this in here?" Jacobi looked around the wagon's interior.

Among the bed, wardrobe, desk, chests, and table with chairs, shelves were lined with musty old tomes. Exotic trinkets that conjured images of weird and unknown things were strewn about, oddities against the flickering light of burning candles. There were a few instances of the same symbol on books and ornaments that hung about Jacobi's neck.

"That's only in your mind's eye," the magician chuckled, twirling his moustache, and waving toward the table. "M'laddo, would you care for some tea?"

Before Jacobi could answer, the cat returned, with Buddy following through the small lower door within the larger door.

"Have you finished playing *bounty hunter* with the canine?" Lafayette smiled.

The black cat raised its head, eyes bright with delight, slinking around Jacobi's leaning crutch before padding under the table.

"That fine creature goes by the moniker of *Memphis*," Lafayette explained. Buddy stayed near the door, panting slightly with his tongue out as though he were smiling.

Memphis leaped onto the bench, Jacobi having not noticed the china teapot there earlier, steam floating from the spout. The strangest thing was, there was no fire to have heated the water and there had been no fire going outside.

"Actually," Jacobi answered, "I'd really like some coffee, if you have it. Hawk gave me some coffee that... I don't know how to explain it."

Charles brought the teapot to the table with two matching patterned china teacups. "Jacobi, we are not common reprobates, and we will not be consuming that putrid broth. Your *Boston Tea*

Party transpired over a century ago and the subsequent revolution was well and truly won. Your Bostonian patriotism against tea is long overdue for retirement."

"I, uh, have nothing particular against tea... I just like coffee."

"We will be drinking tea as civilised gentlemen." The magician studied the familiar charm around Jacobi's neck. "It may not appear so after the Terror Gator attack, but Fate has been kind to you. While you are not the first that Hawk or Alfred Miller have been charitable towards, you are the first to be delivered directly to me in this manner. You also wear Hawk's pendant; a trinket that in the past was most sacred to him." Lafayette poured the tea and handed Jacobi a cup. "Why is that? Tell me everything you know, or think you know..."

Jacobi sipped some tea, surprised by how much he enjoyed the sweet flavour, and began the tale of the mistake of travelling to the West with Francis Geddes.

The magician's piercing blue gaze focused upon Jacobi, much as it had on the steamer.

Then, swallowing too much tea, Jacobi told of those he saw in the sky on the night he fought with his friend. Of when he fell overboard from the paddle steamer into the jaws of the dragon-like monster and was saved by spirits on horses and a thundering bird with barbarian archer at the lead. Then, upon waking in a world that felt far more real, the same man from the dream among the riders had handed him the necklace with the charm of intricate weaved lines.

"That pendant upon your neck; it's symbol is known as *Aetron*. It sets in motion a series of events in the threads of *Fate*, like the turning of a wheel. It tells me our friend sees in you much beyond that which you can see in yourself, whether an inception or a terminus. For this, I am humbled to offer my services to you in the future upon a condition: if ever you feel Fate converging to the point of *doom*."

As Jacobi tried to comprehend just what he meant, the ambient light in the caravan seemed to dim in response as the magician spoke, also just as he thought it had on the *River Grace*.

"The Ghost Riders are tortured souls beyond redemption, cursed with forever pursuing an infernal herd across eternal skies. Legend has it that the riders are a warning, that a time of reckoning is at hand, failure resulting in riding the sky among their great hunt without end."

Lafayette's blue eyes pierced Jacobi's soul. "Why, I do wonder, did you see Hawk among them... And, before all else, why did the Ghost Riders appear to you that fateful night?"

PART II

VENGEANCE

CHAPTER 4

Jacobi was in the frontier cattle town of Sundown. He had himself some hot coffee from a pale stone goblet that the bartender had explained was, "alabaster."

Eating his meal, he found himself wishing that he had some more of Lafayette's tea – or better yet, Hawk's coffee. Jacobi swore that between the magician's brew and Hawk's medicine that he'd recovered from his terrible wounds faster than expected.

Before parting ways for a coach from Mudflats to Sundown, Miller had handed Jacobi some paper money for assisting in the wagon delivery, saying, "People are mostly scared of the Indians, but they'll pay big for their trinkets.

Here's your cut. It's only *proper.*" The veteran had smiled with the last word.

Jacobi was tired and famished from the long coach journey, but after his meal it was time to find new clothes for living in the West. He hadn't had much luck trying to locate Hawk when he wandered around Sundown. He wanted to thank him for saving his life and find out on Miller's behalf if he was about to do something he'd regret.

They were good people he'd met. First the enigmatic Hawk, then the no-nonsense Alfred Miller, and finally the mysterious Charles Lafayette. Jacobi had found himself their welcome stranger in their unwelcoming strange land.

In Sundowner Saloon - or as the locals called it, *The Sundowner* - Jacobi had himself a fantastic view. He was seated at a table close to the piano being played while being able to look out the window across the paddocks, corrals, and pens of Sundown. He dined with pleasure as the warming midday sun passed over the livestock town. For the first time since coming to the West, Jacobi felt relaxed.

Relaxed, that was, until a familiar red and white dog rushed across some paddocks toward the saloon. The red husky was sniffing a trail, most likely Jacobi's scent from the coach station – had Buddy followed the coach through day and night? The dog rushed under the swinging saloon doors towards Jacobi, barking in time with a haunting chant that had become suddenly apparent, a ghostly chorus he'd heard before he fell from the *River Grace*...

"I will wear my hair long." Hawk had walked with deliberate pace from the brush surrounding Sundown, leaving his faithful horse, Blaze, behind to graze on some green grass. Passing some homesteads, he made his way toward the rear of Sundowner Saloon. "I will be known by the name of *my* people."

Hawk's long black hair flowed with eagle feathers behind him. His face was streaked with red and black paint. Bare shoulders were flecked with white dots upon tan skin. A red bird mural was painted across his chest. He was barefoot, the only clothing worn were buckskin pants.

Townsfolk scattered as the savage entered Sundown! It was a rare sight since most of the wild Wakoda Indians had been forcibly removed from the surrounding areas. If the sight of a warpainted savage didn't strike fear into the populace of Sundown, it was the tomahawk in hand. The Indian walked with indomitable steps, ignoring the scattering civilians, and entered one of the rear doors of Sundowner Saloon.

"Hey," a cowboy gasped, "you don't belong!"

"This Fate is not for you." Hawk brushed the man aside, raising the tomahawk. "Do not make it for you."

The cowboy didn't even put a hand to his holstered revolver, instead dropping his drinking glass and running for the door. "Get the Law, there's an Indian in here!"

Hawk made his way up the stairs, passing fleeing patrons as he read the brass plate on each door that he passed. He stopped at the one room he sought above any other.

Hawk had successfully stalked Twyla Matthias undetected for years, to the point where the opportunity to enact vengeance upon her for her crimes would be easily calculated. When the day came, he'd know just where and at what moment to strike. Today, her guards had headed toward the train station, and all signs of opportunity told that the saloon was the place and that the time had arrived.

One of Twyla Matthias' many habits was flaunting her gold and renting rooms, whether saloon or bordello. Loose lips of saloon patrons around Sundown, that weren't aware of an Indian in their midst, had gossiped of "Room 9."

When he reached the room, Hawk smashed the door open, wood splintering around the handle. A man and two women, wearing barely a thread, were with Twyla Matthias.

He pointed the tomahawk with menace at his target to remain but spoke to her guests. "Cover your shame and go with peace," the Indian commanded. They scrambled for as much of their clothing as the most direct route to the door would allow.

Twyla Matthias had already been redressing, adjusting her brunette hair about her bare shoulders. Her usually porcelain face appeared as though she had been in a state of hurried bother before Hawk had arrived. "What is the meaning of this?" she demanded.

"I *was* Thunder Hawk of the Wakoda." The Indian stomped over to the woman as she reached under her scarlet dress for a concealed weapon. "Your greed ends here." He knocked the knife that she had produced from a garter across the room. "For my people that you displaced and the spirits of those you murdered. For the land that you rape for gold that you cannot eat."

"I-I remember you... from the group that refused to move to the Reservation." Twyla raised her hands, attempting to pass the blame for the atrocities committed. "It was Captain Cordell that attacked the Wakoda."

"Funded by your blood-stained gold and need for more!" Hawk swung his axe with the head angled so the blunt flat bulk of the head would be enough to drop the woman to the floor.

He grabbed a clump of tousled hair, dragging his prey from the room to an adjoining doorway that led to the balcony outside.

Most townsfolk near the back of The Sundowner had initially scattered, but some had returned. Others also gathered outside the front in the street, having heard the spreading word about the savage Indian across town, including Jacobi restraining Buddy.

Hawk stood behind Twyla Matthias, facing her to the townspeople, forcing her to her knees at the balcony railing. He then placed the sharp edge of the tomahawk across the top of Twyla's forehead, pressing, drawing blood, ready to scalp the woman that had been a stain upon the land.

He drew his victim's head back enough to gaze into her eyes, to watch the evil slip away when the time came, but Twyla offered no resistance as the sharp edge dug a little further into her scalp.

"What... what are they? Who are they?" Twyla Matthias cried.

Something was vastly different in her eyes, as though she was seeing a terrifying world beyond. The woman's gaze darted around, not at the townsfolk below, but at many things in the air that were not there. "I'm sorry, forgive me..." She didn't possess the terror of waiting inevitably to die; she wasn't even offering any resistance for her life. Twyla peered with horror all about herself, surrounded by a swarm of terrible things greater than the threat of death. "Please," she begged, but not to the Indian, "forgive me for what I have done."

Jacobi had heard them approaching, just as Twyla had before Hawk burst into her room. The Ghost Riders, formless spirits of ghastly men and horses, circled about Sundowner Saloon. They fired guns of smoke and hollered unholy things. Hawk's face had become like a skull, his hair aflame. Burning wings appeared to sprout from the Indian's back as a great storming bird arrived to perch behind him. Jacobi realised that only he and Hawk's victim were witnessing the spectral occurrence.

Hawk held Twyla Matthias as something unknown other than he and the tomahawk continued its torment. She watched her personal angel of death, the demonic visage of the Indian, throw the tomahawk away over the crowd below and release her, unable to continue his personal vendetta, the ethereal hoard disappearing with the weapon.

Not that it would have mattered amongst the folk of Sundown that the Indian had relinquished his assault, but it came all too late as a revolver shot from a lawman running in the street found the Indian's chest.

Sundown deputies burst onto the balcony, overpowering and beating the painted savage as Twyla Matthias continued to cower in terror.

They kicked the Indian back into the saloon and down the stairs. The Law continued the assault as they came out into the street and towards the Sheriff's Office. The people of Sundown threw vegetables at the savage Indian from the displays of market stalls, cussing at him, as he was dragged brutally on.

Jacobi had held Buddy through the ordeal. He dropped his crutch, and with a limp, retrieved the tomahawk before anyone began to care about it. He continued to hold the barking husky's fur outside the crowd, trying to calm him and keep him from going after Hawk – he'd heard how bad it could be to end up on the dog's bad side.

"Go and find Miller." Jacobi held Buddy's fur to face him directly, looking intently into the dog's different coloured eyes. "Do that thing you do. Then bring him back here. Do you understand? Find Miller! Bring Miller here!"

Jacobi looked up at Twyla Matthias cowering from the unseen terrors, nobody able to get close enough to the flailing woman to help her. Twyla shouted to be left alone, going inside and pulling the doors to her room shut.

As Buddy bolted away, Jacobi waded through the crowd trying to reach Hawk. He shoved manic onlookers away. "You can't do this!" he shouted, tomahawk hidden, his voice drowned by the mob.

In time, Jacobi could only stand there, helpless, as Hawk was dragged violently into the Sheriff's Office. The door shut behind, muffling the screams of unnecessary violence.

The young man turned away in defeat. At the other end of the street he could see the golden-tan coat and black-striped legs of Blaze that had brought Hawk here, and that had pulled Jacobi by travois into the West.

The horse had seen the entire ordeal.

CHAPTER 5

In Sundowner Saloon, Room 3, Jacobi had furtively cleaned and hid Hawk's unique weapon in the bottom drawer of the bedside dresser. The Indian axe was strange to him, hollow through the handle to a small bowl-like opening at the poll opposite the blade.

As he closed the drawer, thinking about the days since he'd sent Buddy to find Miller, there was a knock at the door.

"Who is it?" Jacobi asked, not sure who would come knocking for him.

"My name is..." the voice was familiar, pausing before revealing, "...Twyla Matthias..."

Jacobi's skin turned an impossible shade of white. "Uh, I'm not expecting anyone by that name."

"I saw you pick up the Indian weapon."

After the incident with Hawk, he wasn't ready to deal with anything like that just yet. Despite all the madness of almost being scalped and surely witnessing an appearance by the Ghost Riders, Twyla Matthias had somehow managed to see him retrieve the tomahawk and had recognised him. She'd surely used her resources and cunning to find him - his name was signed into Sundowner Saloon's guest registry - and was undoubtedly coming to collect the debt that the dullard Francis had caused. That's twice now his name was easily found; Jacobi realised he really needed to start using an alias in the West.

He opened the door. *Why did I open the door?* He knew he'd probably regret the decision.

If not for her already-established reputation, everybody around The Sundowner at the time of the attempted murder by the savage Indian recognised Twyla Matthias. Without a doubt, the woman who had almost been scalped upstairs outside Room 9 stood at the doorway; lavish red dress, gold-plated revolver holstered, matching red bonnet held in manicured fingers that quivered. "I'm sorry to intrude. May I come in?"

This was not the Twyla Matthias that Jacobi and Francis had faced over the poker table on the *River Grace.*

Sure, her porcelain features had returned and her dark hair was tied perfectly above a medical dressing, but it was the nervous hands that threw Jacobi's expectations off. Everything that he knew about the woman had come from Hawk, Miller, Lafayette and his own experience on the *River Grace* – and not one piece of that information was pleasant.

"Please, do not fear," Twyla pleaded, "I am not here to collect on the debt. In fact, on my behalf, do consider the debt rescinded."

"Why would you do that?" Jacobi pointed to the professional wound-dressing adorning the area where a tomahawk had sliced into Twyla's skin. "Did the axe cut too far into your head?"

"If I may, I'd like to explain everything."

Jacobi looked throughout the hallway for the blue military uniforms of her protective thugs. "Where's your guards?"

Twyla explained. "I relieved them of their contract, stating that the Indian was clever enough to attack me when they were elsewhere in Sundown, so their services were useless to me. I sent them back to their commanding officer where they belong. It was an abuse of my standing to illegally engage the private services of U.S. Army soldiers from that rogue, Captain Cordell, for my own personal needs."

Jacobi had heard that name mentioned before by Miller. Twyla Matthias didn't appear to be the force of personality that he had first met, but perhaps in a good way. Letting go of things such as illegal mercenaries and expensive debts to stupid folk that were caught in a gambling trap - things that were unpleasant about herself.

Wanting to know the fate of Francis after the *River Grace* outweighed Jacobi's not wanting to know. Before he could ask about his absent travelling companion, Twyla explained, "I sent orders to Boom Town... to let your friend go. I had Francis Geddes working off your shared debt to me in the gold mines there. He is free."

Jacobi breathed a sigh of relief, not just in part for himself, but at least knowing that Francis could go home. Convinced of her, Jacobi motioned Twyla inside, closing the door behind.

"Hot coffee?" Jacobi poured the beverage from a pot into the room's second alabaster goblet, handing it to Twyla, motioning for her to sit in a plain wooden chair.

"Thank you."

Jacobi sat on the end of the bed, sipping his own. "It's good and hot, but not as good as a coffee I tasted recently in the wild."

Twyla raised her goblet. "We're all discovering new things here." After tasting the beverage and releasing a smile of delight, Twyla began the story of why she had come to Jacobi.

"The Indian, this *Hawk*, may as well have stripped the scalp from my wicked head for what I have done in my time, especially to him and his people. He hesitated, and I know I risk all sincerity when I tell you this, I'm sure that he hesitated because he knew I was seeing something from Beyond."

Twyla Matthias met Jacobi's eyes, locking his gaze. "You see, Jacobi Nicholson, of Boston, Massachusetts, I could hear *them* approaching before Hawk arrived, before *they* arrived... As that axe you retrieved was brought to my skull, it was then that I saw the spirits of a thousand tortured riders flying from the sky, through my soul, their clarion call so deafening that I can no longer be as I once was. I must follow a better path... we," she motioned towards Jacobi and herself, "must free Hawk, if it's the least I can ever do for him."

A familiar bark sprung Jacobi from his reverie on the front balcony of Sundowner Saloon, the same balcony that had almost been the scene of vengeance.

Thoughts of Twyla Matthias' story of ghostly visitations that saved her life from Hawk's vengeful tomahawk faded from his waking mind. As curious as those strange events certainly were, Jacobi was left wondering why he had witnessed, now for the second time, the

Riders before they made an appearance to the terrified Twyla Matthias.

Jacobi left his chair and leaned on the balcony balustrade to see Buddy signalling, as only a dog can, toward him.

On the worn road alongside the paddocks and pens came the grizzled Alfred Miller driving Maple Stirrup and Sarge on a wagon loaded with barrels.

He'd done it: Buddy had brought Miller to Sundown!

Jacobi rushed down through the hotel as best his healing limp would allow with the crutch. Dodging a passing stagecoach, he reached Miller. "Buddy found you! I hoped he'd understood me when I asked him to bring you here." Jacobi stroked the husky's face, the dog missing him though their friendship had only been short so far.

"He sure did, Jake," Miller answered. "There'd better be a good reason - if Buddy hadn't found me, I'd be in Rosewood about now selling this load of 'shine."

"There is." Jacobi bowed his head. "It's Hawk."

"Fugg, I knew it," Miller sighed. "This good boy has a certain bark and dance of impatience when one of his friends is in trouble. And the word on the trails as I rolled closer to Sundown was that an Indian had tried to scalp Twyla

Matthias with a tomahawk, but he was almost lynched and then thrown behind bars. I guess that means it's all true, and Hawk's revenge failed?"

"He stopped the scalping before the deputies had even got him."

"Why would he stop, when he finally had that fugging bidge's life in his hands?"

"The short version is that Twyla Matthias had a sudden moral epiphany about her life."

"Having an axe to your head'll do that!"

"It wasn't the axe..." Jacobi was sincere. "She saw... *them*..."

"What... I don't believe it. Really?"

"It's true."

"You mean, she saw... *them*, as in...?"

Jacobi nodded, knowing Miller understood. "The Ghost Riders."

Miller shook his head with disbelief as he continued to remove the ropes from the barrels of moonshine.

"I saw them too," Jacobi added, "again."

Miller dropped the ropes with disbelief.

"I could hear them coming, like I did on the *River Grace*. They came for her at that moment before death, and Hawk seemed to understand something was going on with Twyla and spared her. Since then, Twyla Matthias has changed."

"Why would you believe this; how do you know?"

"We met and she told me that she's turned over a new leaf."

"So your new friend Twyla Matthias has seen the Ghost Riders, and you can vouch that fact for her because you saw them as well?" Miller dusted his hat off after the revelation. "You seeing them too is about the only thing that would make me believe she's seen them and changed her ways."

Jacobi let the story sink in some more before adding, "Twyla is in the Sheriff's Office again, trying to get Hawk freed."

"I'll go there too and see what I can do about having a go. Sometimes people have a soft spot for old veterans like me."

"But weren't you with the South?"

"Yeah, but I surrendered and swore allegiance to the Union Army and then fought on the Western Frontier, where I met Sarge here. I just don't tell anyone about the South part," Miller grinned. "Problem is, if all of Twyla Matthias' bribes and clout across this land can't do anything, I'm not sure what I can do."

Miller put his hand on the delivery wagon. "Jake, while I'm gone, I need you to do your best to sell this 'shine to the saloon and get Stirrup and Sarge and the wagon stabled. I'll make sure that no Law comes this way while you make the sale. I can't promise I won't punch Twyla

Matthias in the face if I see her, so that'll be one way I can keep the Law over there."

"Won't somebody at Rosewood eventually want to know where their *'shine* is?"

"Always..." Miller began walking, answering back over his shoulder. "Consider it part of learning how life works here in the West."

CHAPTER 6

Jacobi Nicholson, Alfred Miller and Twyla Matthias sat out on the balcony of the saloon, drinking the new moonshine from Mudflats that The Sundowner had just started serving.

As the three, Twyla included, politely declined the offer from another lady of the night, Miller was weighing the entire situation.

"You've certainly changed, Twyla. You went as far as trying to buy Hawk's life with gold. If not for your welcome interference, he would have probably already swung from the gallows for no other crime than being a fugging Indian. But now they're playing it all by the Law. Before today, I could have happily gunned you down in the street."

Twyla swallowed too much moonshine at the thought. "I am thankful you have not, but was hitting me across the face necessary?"

"You've had more than that coming your way for years," Miller answered, "and it was only to get the Sherriff and his boys' attention away from young Jake here. I am thankful to you for not pressing any charges. But anyway, our bigger issue, we need to explain to Jake."

Jacobi listened attentively.

"We have both run out of time and gained more time. Hawk may have avoided the noose, but the time that has passed has allowed an old enemy of ours, Captain Cordell, to learn of Hawk's capture. The Captain is already outside the limits of Sundown with more troops than we'd be able to count. There's no way we can do any more for him here. Hawk will be escorted by the U.S. Army from Sundown to the Wakoda Reservation up north. But first, Cordell's going to detour east across the Rubicon River with Hawk to get even more troops from Fort Morgan before coming back over the river to then make their way north-west. Cordell has expressly stated that he wishes to escort the prisoner to the Reservation with a show of military force as a message to the Indians there. Hawk is then to remain on the reservation for the rest of his natural life: leaving will instantly put a bounty upon his head; dead or alive."

"I don't like it," Jacobi said. "I'm no soldier, but isn't that overly complicated?"

"I said the same, saying that Hawk could be accompanied by Sundown's Law instead straight to the Reservation land. But this plan is going ahead." Miller wasn't happy. "This is personal for Captain Cordell. He wants to be recorded in history as responsible for conquering the rebellious Indians from these lands."

"Indeed. I know..." Twyla revealed, but adjusted her statement with, "*I knew*... Captain Cordell well."

Miller interrupted. "I served under the fugging bastard, for the Union."

Twyla absorbed that. "I doubt this elaborate plan is for Hawk's safety. In fact, I doubt Hawk will ever reach the Wakoda Reservation. Cordell hates the Indians; he wants to see them conquered."

"Yep," Miller agreed, memories of his past surfacing, "he sure does."

Jacobi put his glass down. "These events, they're all tied together somehow in a way that's bigger than all of us. We need to do something to save him..."

"What, though?" Twyla was listening. "There's no way to spring him from that cell."

"We attack when he's out of the cell, away from Sundown."

"Against the U.S. Army?" Twyla asked.

Miller had an idea. "They have to reach Fort Morgan. They'll need to use the bridge to cross the river. That's when they'll be vulnerable."

"But trapped on the bridge Hawk will probably be at his most vulnerable." Jacobi suggested, "We need a trick; we need a distraction..."

"Oh no..." Miller sighed.

Jacobi was nodding, knowing Miller could sense where he was leading the conversation. "We get more weapons," he knocked his glass over like a chess piece with his revolver, "and we get some help, some real help."

"Uh...who's help?" Miller sighed, knowing he shouldn't have asked.

"Lafayette..." Jacobi placed his revolver on the table where his glass was, "made me a deal."

"*Chuck the magician...?* And some more guns?" Miller was annoyed by the very existence of Lafayette, but he couldn't deny the man's strange abilities.

Twyla curiosity piqued. "Lafayette... as in, *The Charles Lafayette?* The mysterious magician sitting at our poker table on the River Grace?"

"Of course you've fugging met him too," Miller sighed.

Jacobi confirmed. "The very same."

"If Charles Lafayette is what we need," Twyla placed her gold-plated revolver on the table next to the other, "then count me in."

"What?" Miller laughed. "There's no way you're coming."

"And why not?" Twyla demanded.

"Because you're a fugging woman!"

Jacobi raised a hand. "A woman, willing to help us free Hawk."

Miller sank back in his chair, biting his tongue with thought for a moment, then sculled his remaining moonshine. "You win, Jake. If anyone can pull the wool over the eyes of these fugging soldiers, it's Chuck fugging Lafayette."

He nodded at Twyla. "This kid is turning into a real outlaw." Miller put his revolver next to the pair already on the table. "Let's leave Sundown before the army arrives. I know where Chuck will be."

"So, we're doing this?" Jacobi smiled.

Miller put a firm hand on Jacobi's shoulder, nodding. "Yes Jake, we're fugging doing this!"

PART III

CROSSING THE RUBICON

CHAPTER 7

"He's here. I know it. He's just toying with us."
At intersecting roads, a few dozen yards north of
the ruined town of Haven, Miller shook his head
with frustration. "Jake, get me the shovel..."

By the light of the lantern hanging on the
horse-drawn wagon that had been driven from
Sundown, Jacobi rummaged for the shovel. "This
place is giving me the creeps..." The clouds
covering most of the night stars didn't help his
feeling of anxious dread.

Miller smiled. "You don't know the half of
it. Haven isn't called a *ghost town* just because
it's empty... it's *said* to be haunted..."

Jacobi could see the slight silhouettes of
dilapidated buildings under the limited starlight –
they were too close for comfort.

Twyla Matthias put down some water and hay from the wagon for their four horses. Maple Stirrup and Sarge had pulled the wagon while Hawk's horse, Blaze, which Jacobi had stabled after seeing it in Sundown, was tethered to the back. "There you go, Dasher," Twyla stroked her brown and white horse.

Buddy sniffed around to assist Jacobi with finding the shovel as he wondered, "Shouldn't there be that weird caravan-wagon thing of his nearby?"

"You'd be forgiven for thinking so, but this is fugging Chuck Lafayette we're talking about." Miller looked around, not expecting anyone to be passing by as the hour was approaching midnight, but explained what could happen. "Parts of the Frontier, like Haven, are more dangerous than others, especially at night. Run-down old ghost towns are great spots to hide for vagrants and outlaws who should be more scared of what's in there than whatever it is they're running from."

Jacobi brought the shovel over, wondering why the tool was needed. Miller scooped three shovels-worth of dirt from the middle of the crossroads.

While Twyla petted the necks of the eating horses, she asked, "Pardon the intrusion from someone so new to this partnership, but what are you doing? Digging for gold?"

"Chuck's not here, where he last told me he'd be, so..." Miller grinded his teeth, "He's *forcing* me to *summon* him..."

Twyla found that very odd.

"What, why?" Jacobi was confused.

"It's what he does, Jake." Miller grunted. "Otherwise, he wouldn't be able to call himself *The One and Only, Chuck Lafayette, Mythical Mystery Man,* or whatever he is, and all those other strange words that he's concocted."

"Oh," Jacobi responded. When he had met Charles Lafayette the second time, the magician had revealed the nature of the spectral encounter that had plunged him from his previous life into a new path in the West. Everything about Lafayette was indeed strange, mysterious - even terrifying - but the man did seem to know about things that most people would choose not to. "So, what's the hole for?"

Miller reached inside the chest of his rugged coat, unpinning an item. "We each need to sacrifice something of meaning to us." He placed a military medal - browned with age - into the hole. A clasp with a shield held a fabric ribbon of red, white and blue that held an eagle atop crossed cannons on cannonballs from which hung a five-pointed star containing an image of a shield-bearing robed woman defending against a cowering attacker.

"Surely you're not serious?" Twyla lit her fancy city lantern, helping to brighten the crossroads. "What manner of man would make such an... *occult...* request?"

"You should know, you've met him before." Miller breathed a sigh, having been in this situation with the magician before."

"If I'm partaking of this *ritual*, I may as well start believing the tales of *spiderfolk* in the mines of Boomtown."

"What's not to believe," Jacobi reasoned, "when you've seen the *Ghost Riders*..."

Twyla Matthias had to chew on that realisation for a moment. "Checkmate, Mister Nicholson, my king is defeated. Well played."

Jacobi admired the medal resting in the crossroads hole. "I never knew you had a medal. Is it from the war?"

Miller explained, "It's usually well-hidden. Thieves would love to get a hold of it." His thoughts rested for a few moments on his time in the Confederate Army, the senselessness of that slaughter, his eventual betrayal to the side of the Union, his time posted to the Wakoda Indians and the irrationality and violence of their continual relocation. The man he had become since made better decisions, he hoped. He locked eyes with Jacobi. "I don't keep this because I am proud of it. I keep it as a reminder of what I did and didn't do right during the war."

Twyla put her lantern down. She unbuckled a saddlebag upon her horse, scooped a large handful of gold coins, and threw them into the shovelled hole.

"That won't do," Miller stated, flat.

"Not enough? It's valuable."

"Not valuable enough." Miller explained. "While all your coins and baubles have value, they're not valuable to you."

"Why not, gold was very dear to me?"

Miller explained further, "It's no sacrifice to a woman with so much."

"You're absolutely right." This is exactly what Twyla was learning upon the new path in life she had committed herself to.

She dug into another saddlebag and retrieved a round locket on a gold chain. "For many years, I forgot I even still had this." The reforming woman opened it, one side showing a photo of her younger self and the other a young man – they were both happy. She placed it within the hole next to Miller's medal. "This man was my Husband. His want for a simple rancher's life wasn't good enough for me, so I left him, and I soon had control of gold mines. One day the Wakoda attacked the ranch, he was all alone, and they killed him. I sold the land and never cared for Indians thereafter. This locket is now a reminder to never follow that path again."

"That sounds painful." Miller didn't know what else to say. "Jake?"

"I don't have anything that would count. I lost all I had on the *River Grace*. I now have some clothes, a hat, a gun and some friends."

Jacobi gave it some more thought. "Hawk gave me this strange trinket." He held it aloft, the lines of the remaining wood in the carving appearing like a spider's web in the lantern light.

"Did he tell you about it?" Miller asked.

"He said it had belonged to his brother and that I'd learn more when Fate and I found it necessary. Do you know what it is?"

"I think he meant for you to discover most of that for yourself."

Twyla liked that. "Sometimes we have to experience something for ourselves to fully understand its intrinsic value... just like seeing the Ghost Riders."

"You've come far, Jake." Miller smiled. "A lot of what Hawk says doesn't make sense at the time, but often leads to something when you least expect it. Stranger things like that are traces of the man he used to be before ending up with the likes of me. You know, we three wouldn't even be here, together, trying to find Lafayette, if not for your insistence to do something more drastic than just talking to the Law. Twyla and I would probably still be arguing against deaf ears in Sundown, to the point where they'd lock us both up for disturbing the peace."

Miller agreed with the item. "I say toss it in, Jake."

"Yes indeed," Twyla also agreed.

Jacobi wasn't sure. "What if Hawk wants it back, or if he wants to give it back to his brother?"

"This is the West. You can meet a man in a town and then never see him in that town ever again. Things are usually given for keeps." Miller was assuring. "But, he gave that to you before he set out abruptly to scalp Twyla in Sundown."

Twyla's eyes lit with shocking memory.

"I'd assume, going into a white man's town as a red man to kill a prominent white woman, he wasn't expecting to be alive for long after," Miller explained. "I'd guess it's all part of that *Fate* that Lafayette harps on about. I don't try to understand it."

Jacobi thought about everything Hawk and Lafayette had told him. Instilled with the mysterious nature of his time in the West, he placed the charm necklace among the medal and the locket.

Miller shovelled the hardened earth of the crossroads back into the hole on top of their items, Buddy inspecting the work with meticulous sniffing.

As Miller pressed on the dirt with his boot to pat the soil down, Jacobi asked, "Now what?"

Twyla was stroking the blaze of her horse. "Perhaps this mysterious showman wants us to cast a heathen *spell* of some sort?"

"Don't joke, that's just the sort of thing he'd pull on us." Miller groaned. "Now we wait for as long as that fugging shyster wants us to wait."

"This *Charles Lafayette*," Twyla adjusted a shawl over her outfit, her usual dresses left behind in Sundown, replaced by the shirt and pants of a cowboy, "is he a rather trying individual?" She looked at her gold pocket watch, seeing that it was two minutes to midnight.

"You mustn't have spent long enough in his company." Miller went and stood beside the crossroads.

"How *real* is this *summoning*?" Twyla asked. "It's all just tricks and bunkum with magicians, isn't it?"

"As strange as it sounds, anything magical or mystical," Miller explained, "are the only things that seem real about Chuck."

"How long will he make us wait?"

The question was answered by the gurgling croak of ravens all around.

Buddy's ears pricked and he barked in response, defensive. Jacobi eased him, stroking his fur, "Easy, Buddy."

Twyla kept the four horses calm, cooing.

Miller frowned. "Ravens..."

Jacobi reiterated, "I said this place was creepy." He reached for his holstered gun, Twyla doing the same.

Miller held a hand out for them to stop, explaining, "It's either every raven in the area is here or it's one of Chuck's tricks." He asked Twyla, "What time is it?"

She raised an impeccable eyebrow. "I would like to say it's *time for you to get a pocket watch*, but, it is coincidentally... just passing the stroke of... midnight."

"I bet it's Chuck." Miller shook his head. "Ravens are like his symbol of death or something."

"How theatrical," Twyla intoned.

"Exactly," Miller agreed. "But in case we get swarmed, keep those hands near your weapons."

Jacobi pointed, suddenly noticing that, "There's a light over there... Coming from inside a... looks like, like, like a church? There wasn't any light shining over there before..."

From inside one of the better-standing abandoned buildings, of what was left of the town of Haven, a warm light was shining from inside boarded windows. The three travellers assured themselves that the light wasn't there during the waiting at the crossroads.

Armed with a lantern each and a hand near their firearms, leaving their horses behind, Jacobi, Miller and Twyla stepped carefully toward Haven. The croaking of surrounding ravens and the town's haunted reputation made the three uneasy, including their dog following.

Twyla looked at Jacobi. "Are you travelling well?"

Jacobi swallowed. "I'd rather be back in the mouth of that big Terror Gator..."

"Well," Miller almost chuckled, "alligator territory isn't that far away; Mudflats is east..."

Jacobi was shaking, quietly muttering, "Nope, nope, nope. Not helping at all..."

Buddy ran ahead, toward the light.

Jacobi swallowed a yell, "Buddy, back!"

The three had to step faster after the husky, their own illumination revealing the boarded-up church with rows of tombstones nearby among other broken buildings of the abandoned town.

The tombstones were many, their rows disappearing into the edge of darkness that the lanterns couldn't shed light upon. Before any of the three could even read an epitaph, a voice from inside the church saved them the time.

"The Battle of Haven was a fortunate and unfortunate time for its residents during the Civil War... those that died were spared the further horrors that followed; an unearthly disease and a native internment camp to name only a few."

"Chuck..." Miller muttered under his breath.

Jacobi was the first to notice, "That entry was boarded up only moments ago..."

Sure enough, the entrance to the church was open to the world as though it had never been boarded closed. A single door still hung from a damaged hinge while light poured from inside.

As the three companions moved closer to the door, they recognised Charles Lafayette at a round table with a soft green cover, four pews facing inward around it. He faced them, his calm black cat sitting next to him.

Buddy – the animal no longer alert against the ravens – sat up, peering happily, on a pew to the magician and feline's left. The remaining two pews were empty, despite cards having been dealt on the table before the pew across from Lafayette. It appeared as though he and his cat were playing poker against an empty seat. At the centre of the table rested a familiar medal, locket and charm - all perfectly clean.

"What the fugg, Chuck!" Miller was exasperated. "You could have just called us over..."

"And deny you the sweet lullaby of a conspiracy of ravens?"

"Are there ravens out there or is it just you?"

Lafayette simply twizzled his moustache, a coy smile upon his un-answering face.

Twyla stepped forward. "Excuse me, but those possessions are ours?" This was definitely the magician she and Jacobi played poker with on the *River Grace*.

"M'Lady, Twyla Matthias, we meet again, if not for the first time or the last. You are, however, correct at this point in time, but moments ago those possessions were not yours."

"What are you suggesting?" Twyla was taken aback. "That locket has always been mine."

"The valiant Memphis, here," Charles leaned his head, the wide brim of his hat patting the black cat's head, "just won your sacrificial effects back against all odds."

Jacobi swore the black cat looked proud of itself as its head was touched, if such a thing were possible. The bright yellow eyes even conveyed a certain level of smugness. He was afraid to ask, "From whom?"

"The lost souls of Haven, of course."

"Lost souls?" Jacobi just had to ask.

"Yes, M'laddo. Don't you feel the hairs standing up on the back of your neck?" Charles grinned. "That's them..."

The sound of ravens faded, enhancing Jacobi's fears as he sidestepped himself to look around for people that weren't there. "Well, I definitely do now!"

"If you're done with your pretentious show," Miller went for the empty pew across from Lafayette and Memphis, "we've come to talk…" He sighed. " *We* want your help."

"Don't sit there," Lafayette warned. "They don't like it when you sit *in* them. And… *pretentious?* One could take offence at such an adjective," the magician smirked, "but I'm rather more impressed with the fact that you possess this modicum of such language. Miller, as they say in the saloons, my good company must be *rubbing off on* you."

"Unlikely," Miller rolled his eyes at the suggestion as he sat next to Buddy while Jacobi and Twyla sat across from them – the pew across from Lafayette remaining physically unoccupied.

Miller breathed his frustration. "Can you help us. Hawk has been taken prisoner. Captain Cordell is about to surface again. He's going to move him via U.S. Army escort from Sundown to the Wakoda Reservation, permanently."

"It's that last part we don't believe," Jacobi added.

"Jacobi Nicholson. M'laddo… look at you." Charles smiled. "You've gone and got yourself a splendid hat and spinning spurs, lost the dandy clothes of the East, and keep itching to reach for your shiny new revolver. If I'm not mistaken, the man that Fate had fall from grace to land in the

West is becoming a real-life outlaw. Careful you don't fall too far, *Jake*..."

"Well..." Jacobi didn't know how to respond. "Why did you call... how did you know Miller calls me *Jake*?"

"Are you willing to shoot a man with that?" The magician glanced to Jacobi's gun belt.

"If I have to... to free Hawk, I would."

"You have changed, indeed, M'laddo." The magician thought a moment. "Jake the Outlaw, if you want my help," Charles Lafayette began returning their sacrificial items, which were cleaner than before they were buried, "I need to know that you are willing to do what it takes. This will be a battle, not just a duel between two desperados in the street. Your mortality is at stake. One of you, all of you, may die – you may fail. Souls will rise and souls will burn. Just make sure that if you spin Fate, you are ready to weave it beyond the consequences."

There was a certain realisation around the poker table in the crumbling church at Haven. This had become very real. What they were planning was outright against the law of the land and involved mortal danger. Their very lives hung in the balance.

The magician continued. "You know what unites us, but you barely speak of it, as though you would be considered insane, even among those that have shared the same ethereal experience. Fate has chosen to unite us, all in a different manner, by our visions of the Ghost Riders."

Twyla tested her scepticism of the magician. "How would you even know what we have seen?"

Miller rolled his eyes. "Don't ask."

"You've seen them too?" Jacobi asked, looking at Miller and then the magician. He sensed that Lafayette must have seen them, whether that was how he gained his esoteric knowledge about them or not, but he never told of it when they met - and Miller was just the sort of man that would keep such things tightly locked until he knew you well enough.

"More times than you could fathom, M'laddo," Charles bowed his brimmed head. "My dreams, both waking and not, are the fabric of nightmares. But this is because I do not adhere to the mantra of *follow no dreams.*"

The magician raised his head. "But, did you know, the man you wish to free has not witnessed the Ghost Riders for himself?"

"He hasn't?" Jacobi was stunned. He had assumed Hawk had seen them somewhere in his past, because he believed Jacobi's sighting without hesitation. After the Indian had heard his tale about the Ghost Riders, and the way Jacobi saw him riding upon a thundering bird among them, Hawk had sent him to meet

Lafayette and learn about them. "So, what does that mean?"

"It doesn't change anything," Miller interrupted. "Hawk believes that we have seen them, and that's all that's ever mattered to him - it has always been enough for him."

Twyla agreed, "I concur. It shouldn't change anything."

Jacobi answered Lafayette. "What better reason is there than simply to free a man that will be murdered for being a product of trying to live by the way of his people as a world he didn't ask for continued to force his Fate in this... this *West*. As strange as it is, we each seeing the Ghost Riders has brought us together around Hawk's Fate."

With a proud smile, Lafayette asked Jacobi, "Do you sense something in Hawk's Fate?"

"When we met, you offered your services on a condition." Jacobi held aloft the charm of the feather-adorned necklace. "I feel that Hawk's fate is headed towards that condition." Jacobi brought forth an aspect of his deep conversation with the magician. "I feel that his Fate is converging to the point of doom..."

CHAPTER 8

Wearing blue uniforms, they came for him in the dead of night. No warning, abrupt, using the terror of being torn from sleep as a weapon. Under the cover of darkness, the Indian prisoner was removed from the confines of Sundown and forced to march toward his impending doom.

During the quiet moments, Twyla Matthias would occasionally insert a spark of words to ignite a conversation during their journey.

"Have either of you two ever heard of the term, *Deus ex Machina?*"

She did worry that Miller either was not interested in anything she had to say or much of her words were beyond his comprehension.

Miller rode shotgun, looking back over the sight of supply crates, weapons and ammunition that had mysteriously appeared in their wagon after meeting with Lafayette. Twyla rode her horse beside their two-horse wagon, Jacobi at the reigns, Hawk's horse following freely behind. The red husky explored the trail ahead.

Still developing his skill driving the two-horse wagon, Jacobi found the course that had been laid out for them from the ruins of Haven to the dreaded Fort Morgan to be increasingly difficult. But according to Lafayette, it would *cause as little vibration in the Web of Fate as possible to avoid detection until the time of opportunity presented itself.*

"So, what is a..." Jacobi wondered, "*day-us-ecks-mack-in-uh* or whatever you called it?"

"Deus ex Machina..." Twyla began, delighted for the opportunity to have an educated conversation. "It began centuries ago, used in theatrical performances."

Miller snorted. "Sounds like something Lafayette would like to hear about if he were here."

"Indeed," Twyla agreed, adjusting her gold-rimmed spectacles. "It was a device used by storytellers to often solve a narrative, by inserting a divine character, such as a god, to fix everything: *magic-poof-solved.* The machine was the device that lowered the divine being onto the stage. It sometimes went against any logic built during the story, robbing the audience of everything they had learned to believe or disbelieve so far. But what I find most interesting, just lately in my life, is the term translated - it means, *God from the Machine*.

Miller asked the question Jacobi was thinking. "Why does that catch your attention?"

"Imagine, Gentlemen, if you will, the world as a stage - a machine, and we are the characters. Events have weaved our destinies together, like we are all trains on separate tracks that are merging into each other."

Jacobi raised the charm from his chest, Miller also seeing it. The two of them understood that something unknown was at work, from Hawk to Lafayette, to Twyla's own words. Fate was leading them all somewhere.

"During this," Twyla continued, "against our understanding of all that we knew before, enters that which removes all we previously understood of our own narratives..."

Jacobi and Miller looked at each other, admitting together out loud what Lafayette had made them realise that they didn't speak enough of for fear of being considered insane: "The Ghost Riders..."

Pleased, Twyla tipped her riding bonnet. "Exactly."

The timing was perfect for Captain Phileas Cordell of the United States Army. The prisoner transfer was of his own meticulous design. It was not created to obey the laws of any man, but instead higher powers that most could not understand or dare to comprehend - higher powers that he continued to gain favour with.

The protocol established between the Sundown Sheriff's Office and the La Grande Bureau of Indian Affairs was but a trifle detail in the Captain's scheme. Those institutes wanted the prisoner escorted from Sundown by armed guard to keep the townsfolk calm. Then to Fort Morgan in the East to acquire more soldiers to help protect the transfer for when it went back north-west. It would then travel to the Wakoda Reservation to deliver the prisoner. But that was those institutes' plans, not Cordell's.

Those few loyal to Cordell's sense of defeating the Indians in the West at all costs understood that their prisoner would not survive the night inside Fort Morgan - it was very easy to kill a prisoner and stage the incident as a failed escape attempt.

Those fewer loyal to Cordell by powers from beyond this world understood that the prisoner would never reach Fort Morgan, but instead was doomed to die to a higher purpose.

Phileas Cordell rode at the head of the two by ten long procession of cavalry, followed by ten horse-drawn wagons filled with sitting infantry. His beaten Indian prisoner tried to keep pace on foot, wrists bound and tethered to one of the rear cavalry horses. The prisoner hadn't even been brought before the Captain, just simply dragged, stumbling, behind.

"Speaking of subjects that we don't broach often," Twyla inquired, "it would appear that you have seen the Ghost Riders yourself, Miller, but I have not had the pleasure of hearing the tale... Unless, of course, it is a private matter?"

As Jacobi guided the horses, he looked straight at the side of Miller's weathered face. "Either have I..."

"It's never really come up, and I would have eventually told young Jake here the story, but I have no worries telling it to you both now."

Miller began. "You know I fought in the *War Between the States*. I was conscripted into the Confederate Army, forced to fight for something that I didn't believe in. I was taken prisoner, easily - as I couldn't bring myself to actually shoot to kill a North soldier - and then swore allegiance to the Union Army. I became what they called a *galvanised yankee*. From then on, I fought for the northern states on the Western Frontier, away from any real battles between the states."

The man swallowed, stroking his beard. "I was placed under the command of the infamous *Captain Phileas Cordell*. Like any Union soldier, the man didn't trust ex-Confederates. And even though he was a Union man, he would often express to us that *we had failed the cause*, as though he had interest in the Confederate states winning." Miller shook his head.

"He especially didn't like people like me who didn't blend into his army's culture of superiority. He was so against anyone that didn't have white skin or fit his idea of a *true* American. He never really fought to free slaves and his campaigns were mostly directed against what was referred to as the *Indian problem*. He always claimed to be fighting for a higher purpose and hoped the war between North and South continued as it gave him the ability to fight on the frontier without much oversight from superiors."

"I'm sorry to have known and dealt with the man," Twyla interjected, "but you saw a side of Cordell that I only saw the surface of. I knew he wasn't right in the head, and sadly that was to my advantage."

"I always thought that he was sick in the head," Miller added, "like he just enjoyed the killing and didn't want it to stop. But, there was something deeper in him, a grand design to it all."

"How did you fit into it all?" Jacobi asked.

"I really didn't," Miller answered. "Eventually, to get rid of me, he assigned me to the relocation of the last groups of Wakoda Indians to the Reservation that had been created for them."

Jacobi watched Miller's eyes lower with memory. "I could tell you everything that went wrong, but you'd be listening for days, so for the matter of the Ghost Riders, it begins and ends with a young girl, not even ten years old. In our language, her name was *Little Flower*. She had been given a puppy by the name of *Buddy*."

Miller caught Jacobi's surprised glance. "That's right, Jake. Our Buddy, when he was nothing more than a ball of red fluff, was given to Little Flower by Hawk's half-brother - Roy always did love animals."

"Half-brother, Roy? Do you mean his brother, Royce?"

Miller was surprised Jacobi had been told the name. "Well, the old bounty posters always had listed him as *Royce "Red Roy" Falco*, and they only shared the same mother; Roy's father, Oskar Falco, being a bigtime German railroader."

"I knew Oskar Falco," Twyla admitted.

"Of course you did," Miller sighed.

"Oh," Jacobi nodded, listening intently, looking ahead to Buddy. The red husky carried his own history. He watched the dog assume it was leading the wagon as it found countless things to sniff along the way.

"Little Flower had lost her parents to bandits," Miller continued. "The remaining Wakoda continued to raise her, especially Hawk."

"Our Hawk?" Jacobi asked, as Twyla dealt with inner turmoil arising from newer parts of a story that she knew that she was responsible for.

"The same." Miller remembered. "In those days, he was known as *Red Hawk*, and had lost many people that were close to him - some very close - to the War Between the States that his people had nothing to do with, to settlers going West, to bandits, to relocation, but he wasn't broken by any of it... yet."

Twyla dabbed her eyes with a kerchief that hung around her neck.

"He had a rebellious fire, but he was a very spiritual man. All his life Red Hawk had visions of a Thunderbeing that kept his spirit strong."

Jacobi had to interrupt. "When I saw the Ghost Riders, I saw Hawk among them, riding a giant bird, shooting lightning!"

"Why do you think he had me take you to Chuck the showman?" Miller smiled at Jacobi before elaborating. "All his life, he dreamed that a giant bird was flying toward him, its wings beating with the sound of thunder, and lightning shooting from its eyes. Apparently, it's what was painted on his chest," Miller glanced at Twyla, "before he went for your scalp."

Twyla passed a hand over the area.

"Such visions of a Thunderbird among the Wakoda led him to become a *Spiritwalker*... like a medicine man, a holy man. So Red Hawk led his group in a sort of," Miller tried to conjure the right words, "*spiritual* resistance. They were a group of families in continued defiance of the white man, planting their *tipis* away from the lands they had lost but not going to the reservation. How could they go wrong when they had a Spiritwalker among them? They even called him *Thunder Hawk,* in honour of the Thunderbird he embodied..."

Miller's head bowed. "But, soon enough, the white man wanted to mine for gold on their very camp. I continued to do my duty; I had become friendly, I negotiated Indian Officers visiting, I tried to convince the Wakoda to comply, to do what was in their best interest. But it was the same story, over and over for them, time and again: *that piece of land you're on, you must move, we want it.* And when they didn't move, that's when the army came... and I didn't fight for either side... I remember Roy was visiting and he fought, covered in the blood of soldiers, while I didn't.

"I sadly remember that day..." Twyla Matthias took a turn to bow her head. "They came with Captain Cordell at their head, my disgraceful self not far behind. I may as well have paved the way with bricks of gold, for that is what I paid Captain Cordell and his loyal soldiers to get the job done by any means necessary. Today I am ashamed, that path of gold leading to the Indian camp became stained with blood. The Wakoda fought back with Thunder Hawk: guns, bows, axes, their bare hands, on foot, on horseback... it was no use, though - half of them were slaughtered."

Miller's eyes welled. "There's an abandoned mine there, still to this day."

"There was nothing in the land but a few gold nuggets for the greed of men. I even sold the mine to a desperate settler afterwards for more than it would have been worth." Twyla had to clean the fog from her spectacles. "Where were they taken, Alfred?"

Miller hated his first name being used but didn't even realise that it had been just as Twyla hadn't realised that she had used it.

"Haven, an Indian internment camp was set up in the ruins of the town."

"Haven?" Jacobi was connecting histories. "The camp that Lafayette mentioned?"

"There's a thousand terrible things that have happened in Haven since it was founded," Miller answered. "It wasn't important enough at the time to explain further, and that place already had you shaking in your little cowboy boots."

Jacobi agreed. He wondered about that accursed town. Haven; *how could such a place be the site of so many terrible things.*

"Roy was tried and convicted. He was a real outlaw, a real fugging Wild West gunslinger, with countless bounties on his head as well as having just fought the US Army. His connected father managed to make sure that he only saw the inside of a prison rather than the gallows. Cordell didn't have me discharged for trying to keep the peace during the battle, instead assigning me to oversee the rehabilitation of the Wakoda. Let me tell you both, it was more of a punishment than being discharged and he knew I would feel it that way. His entire method of command seemed based on causing the most misery to others. I regret every day of overseeing the rehabilitation. They assimilated them, especially the children, cutting their hair, forbidding them to speak their own language, and forcing them to take American names. It was Hell on Earth. Many died from starvation, being overworked, no heat. The only saving grace, if it can be called that despite all the other afflictions, was that disease hadn't become a problem."

It was Miller's turn to wipe his eyes, his sleeve passing over his face. "This absolute horror continued until Little Flower died, Buddy howling to the sky in her lifeless arms... Something had been dying in Thunder Hawk since his imprisonment and it finally died with Little Flower. That something in his eyes - the Thunderbird, the Spiritwalker - both gone, replaced by a spirit of vengeance."

"I've seen those eyes." Twyla passed her fingers again over her tomahawk scar, seeing that Miller understood.

"As I stared upon those Wakoda that remained, Thunder Hawk's fists curled, and the sky... I don't know how to describe it other than... it opened up, a storm bursting upon the ruins of Haven and especially upon the internment camp." Miller caught his breath as he finally reached the further unbelievable part of his story. "To this day, Hawk says he never saw them, but neither did anyone else. But I tell you, I did, I saw them. They just appeared, ghostly horseman, riders on the storm, herding fiery cattle. They descended upon the internment camp as the Indians began to revolt."

There was a pause that Jacobi needed to end. "What happened next?"

"One of the riders flew by, as if he knew me, he called to me, *Alfred, Alfred Miller.* Nobody calls me *Alfred.* He told me to finally do what was right, or join them herding the hellish stampede forevermore... I had a standard issue rifle in my hand and a crossroads of a decision in my head: serving my country and serving the Wakoda were not the same – I needed to choose which was right.

The seconds that Jacobi and Twyla waited for Miller to continue felt like years.

"I said fuggoff to the army. I killed my first soldier that day, and not the last. By the time Thunder Hawk and I were done, the Ghost Riders had gone and the internment camp at Haven was a burned husk of bad memories. Not one soldier lived to tell the tale that I had turned against them. Thunder Hawk and I escaped the area, taking the remaining Wakoda - the living and the dead - to their Reservation. Fate, Thunder Hawk said, no matter how much they tried to resist, was dooming the Wakoda to life on the Reservation. But, Thunder Hawk refused to live there, vowing that he couldn't rest until Twyla Matthias and Phileas Cordell paid for their crimes, even if it took years. He went back into the plains of his people, continuing to raise Buddy, never forgetting what happened. Since that day, he tells me that he has not seen his thundering Spiritbird again, and dropped that part of his name, becoming simply *Hawk* – like I told you, they finally killed something in his very spirit that day, and it has never returned. I, hopefully, would be presumed dead as no soldiers survived the battle at the camp. I now live with the land, a trapper and hunter, only using my time in the Civil War when it offers an advantage in lawful society. Hawk and I would often meet, as little as days or as long as months apart, Buddy often our line of communication. We've never seen Roy again. Hawk never doubted my seeing the Ghost Riders, and because of them we made a different life apart from the world of civilisation that keeps coming West."

Miller finished. "These things had been this way until you, Jake, fell from a boat and into our lives, having also seen the Ghost Riders."

Passing the Wakoda Oil Fields, named because it was where a group of the Wakoda Indians had been forcibly removed years earlier, filled Captain Cordell with a sense of pride and power.

East of Sundown, north of Mudflats, west of Rubicon River, the smokestacks belched their black plumes. The thick smoke was accompanied by the industrious wrenching and clanging of oil being drawn from the earth.

The oil fields were one of the biggest signs that the modernising industrial world of the East was intruding into the wild frontiers of the West.

The Captain could have simply put most, if not all, of his men on board a train from Sundown that would have passed by the Wakoda Oil Fields and over the Rubicon River eastward. But Cordell wasn't going to afford the luxury of modern transport to his Indian prisoner. As far as he was concerned, Cordell was forcing the last rebellious Indian of the Haven Indian Internment Camp massacre to be confronted by the progress of civilisation that had been made since forcing his people to scatter from this land.

Now all that remained was his final plan for this Indian.

CHAPTER 9

There it is, Jake, in all its glory," Miller declared, passing his worn binoculars to Jacobi so that he could also get a better look. *"Rubicon Crossing."*

Twyla looked through her own brass-rimmed binoculars. "That magnificent bridge is considered to be the point of no return, connecting the civilised *modernity* of the East to the wild *frontier* of the West." She was glad to be almost resting after days of following Lafayette's mysterious directions through some rugged trackless regions.

Jacobi gazed at the massive metal truss bridge through the binoculars, steel arches and beams appearing like a silver web of industry. It stretched from a cliff edge in the East, spanning incredibly high over the southward rushing waters of the ginormous Rubicon River to meet another cliff edge in the West. The Rubicon Crossing was a marvel of American civilisation and engineering, allowing movement into the West by road and rail. "Coming from Boston, I thought I had seen it all. The frontier continues to impress me."

Jacobi couldn't help but notice that the bridge's design was oddly reminiscent of the necklace that Hawk had given him and that a few ravens were perched atop the structure.

"Gentlemen," Twyla politely interrupted, "I think it's about to become much more impressive..."

Miller grabbed his binoculars back from Jacobi, looking to where Twyla spoke of. To the west of the bridge approached a procession of blue-uniformed soldiers riding beside a railroad on a worn dusty road.

"That's gotta be Cordell at the lead with the captain's rank," Miller stated, having not seen the man in years. "None of the horses are branded, though, they're not U.S. Army property."

Twyla had been studying the leader also, the captain sitting atop a healthy steel-grey horse, her memory of a fruitful partnership now filled her with revulsion. "He often spoke of a *Higher Power*, that *America's Manifest Destiny and the gods of the white, black, brown, yellow and red were just pawns in a cause that dwindled in comparison.* He knew people in high places, that I could be sure of, but there was always something sinister - something hidden - about this Higher Power. He did unusual, peculiar things, disappearing at night, absent on long journeys, able to call in favours from unexpected places, avoiding where possible anything that registered his name. These horses for example: would have been bought with blood money away from the records of the army, his way of keeping some of the extent of his force unregistered. It keeps whatever his clandestine activities are unknown. But, with regards to his identity, I can vouch that that lily-looking officer is definitely Cordell."

Miller handed the binoculars back to Jacobi, the young man chortling. "Look at him. What's with the lady's hair?" He quickly realised what he had said, looking to Twyla and her bun of brunette hair behind bonnet with apology, the usually long hair bound instead for travelling in the wild. "Sorry..."

"Not at all," Twyla smirked. "It's how we of the more *upper-crust* of society flaunt ourselves. Why some men, like Cordell, had to take it that step further, I'll never understand."

Cordell brushed his long curling spirals of blonde hair over his shoulder with a gloved hand, then pressed his thick moustache flatter to his face. He was king of an almost-rogue group of soldiers with the frontier of the West as theirs for the taking as they pleased.

"There's Hawk!" Miller spotted the beaten Indian prisoner at the rear of the cavalry. "We can't even try here. There's so many soldiers that there won't be any room for Hawk to move on the bridge. We'll have to wait until they're over it, follow ourselves, and prepare an ambush.

The beaten Indian prisoner, wrists glistening red from the rope that bound him, was led like one of the horses before Captain Cordell. Hawk finally saw, face-to-face, the one responsible for commanding so much of the destruction to the spirit of his people.

Phileas Cordell ignored the prisoner, barking orders. "Send a scout, reconnoitre further along the tracks east, make sure a train is not coming this way. I don't want civilian eyes anywhere near this area. Watch the northern and southern trails at either end. I don't want any mountain men or this prairie worshipper's Indians" – he now regarded Hawk – "coming this way. Nobody is to get through here until we are clear of the bridge."

The soldiers complied, scurrying about. The cavalry entered first, Cordell at their lead with the horse with the prisoner now beside him. The wagons, with their crates of ammunition, provisions and other supplies, each waited their turn to enter the bridge single-file beside the railroad tracks.

Captain Cordell checked his pocket watch, then addressed the prisoner for the first time, with enough pompous volume that many of his soldiers could also hear. "I'm not going to even dignify you with an attempt at pronouncing the name you refused to give up. The orders, though, officially state your name as *Thunder Hawk*, but that is just a translation of your prairie critter-speak."

Hawk kept stepping with the pace of the horse he was bound to, eyes remaining lowered to the bridge, unmoved.

"What was the name given to you at the Haven Indian Internment Camp?"

Hawk remained solemn, unyielding.

Cordell waved a gloved finger.

A soldier struck the Indian across the face with the butt of a rifle.

"Again," Cordell asked, "what was the name they gave you at the Haven Indian Internment Camp? And remember, we speak *American* here."

Hawk looked up at Cordell, the Captain's face bringing years of pain back to his mind. But he walked with defiance against the question.

The scout returned, saluting, delivering the news, "Captain, no sign of approaching trains ahead."

"Excellent." Cordell didn't return the salute. "Join the ranks."

As the scout fell in line with the cavalry, the Captain's attention reverted to the Indian. "Still, no answer?"

Cordell turned to his closest soldier as they slowly rode. "Give me your service revolver."

Without hesitation, the soldier handed his superior the weapon.

Cordell emptied the chambers, the bullets falling to the tracks. He held the weapon to Hawk. "Take this."

Cordell could see there was going to be no compliance. The Captain kicked Hawk in the gut.

While the Indian was curled over, Cordell dismounted, holding the procession that had wholly made it on to the bridge.

He thrust the revolver into the waist of Hawk's buckskin pants and cut his ropes free with a strange jagged knife, the blade formed of a strange silver weave. "Now, *Savage*, march ahead..." He turned to some of his soldiers. "Remain here. If he runs away from me, shoot him."

Jacobi wanted to know, "Why is Hawk just taking this?"

"There's got to be well-more than fifty soldiers about," Miller answered. "There's not much he can do."

"Yeah," Jacobi nervously agreed, "but if we also don't do anything, it may end up being too late. I've only learned guns recently, but I know what itchy trigger fingers are – and I've got itchy trigger fingers right now."

"As cryptic as his small amount of details were about providing a distraction," Twyla added, "Lafayette said to *wait for a sign.*"

Miller answered, "Whilst I find the antics of Chuck Lafayette fugging infuriating, the man has a mysterious way of providing what we have needed at the right times. I have never felt more ridiculous wearing these belts of ammunition or changing to those bullets with Lafayette's strange mystical symbols etched on them, but I'm sure the magician has provided them for another of his inexplicable setups that I am assuming will pay off again and leave me dumbfounded."

"It better happen soon, we're running out of time." Jacobi didn't mind the ammunition belts, or the extra guns and bullets, at all – all of which had mysteriously appeared in their wagon after enlisting the assistance of the magician. The symbol etched upon each of Lafayette's bullets was the same as Hawk's charm. The three of them looked armed and dangerous, ready for anything.

The matter now, was the timing of when to strike to free Hawk. Over fifty soldiers versus three about-to-be-outlaws of the West. Jacobi wondered if they were going to succeed or be shot down in a blaze of glory. "I still don't get why Hawk isn't doing anything. Is he waiting for Fate to doom him or something?"

As Hawk was walking over Rubicon Crossing, from further eastward came a metallic squeal.

A small red, blue and black railcar rolled along swiftly.

Soldiers armed their rifles, Cordell keeping his knife ready for potential danger and barking, "I thought you said there weren't any trains coming?"

The scout was pale. "There weren't any, Captain, I assure you."

"I don't believe it..." Miller gave the binoculars to Jacobi. "*He's* on the other side of the bridge standing on top of his caravan. Is *this* the fugging sign?"

Twyla answered Jacobi's question of "What?" with "It's Charles Lafayette!"

Sure enough, standing upon his wagon of red, blue and black, as it coasted slower along the rails, was a man decked out in a lavish tailored midnight blue suit. His showy caravan may have traded wagon wheels for those used by trains, but it still showed no signs of how it was actually propelled – no horses, no pumping mechanism, no steam boiler.

As the caravan came to a perfect stop, the new arrival pulled out a handled cone and raised the smaller end to his moustached lips under his overly-wide-brimmed hat. "Step right up, folks, come one, come all," the magician began, booming louder beyond what could be expected of the cone, "may I introduce myself..."

Captain Cordell waved for the magician's attention. "Pardon me, you'll need to move from the tracks. Take your..." he couldn't see how the thing moved, "train... and go back the way you came immediately or be charged with treason. This is United States Army business."

Lafayette removed the cone away from his mouth. "Never interrupt the man with the speaking-trumpet or the show won't go on!"

Putting the contraption back to his lips, and while climbing down one-handed, he continued his broadcast. "I am the One and Only, Charles Lafayette, Legendary Mysterioso, Illusionist, Magician, Perceptivist, Master of Cosmology, Esoterica, Fortuna, Portentia and Mysticism... at your service." The magician struck a proud legs-parted, crossed-arms and chin-raised pose before Captain Cordell.

The Captain pointed his knife, to which the magician remarked of the blade, "A silk weave of unseen folk among webs?"

"You couldn't know of such things... The threat of treason will be raised to death if you don't back away now." Cordell looked over the magician's face. "I'm not usually in the habit of giving your kind second chances, so I suggest you get on board your little train and get out of here."

Lafayette ignored the veiled insult with the practiced grace of an actor, lowering the cone and raising an eyebrow. "But Captain, you don't know what I've come to know. From spiders to nightmares. I do not fear death. Although, you and I must catch that particular train one day. Speaking of which - you may want to miss the next train..."

"Next train?" Cordell was befuddled by the magician.

Lafayette caught sight of Hawk. "Well, I'll be... That Indian you have there, good Captain, I believe I know him."

The Captain raised his weapon closer to Lafayette's face. "You do?"

"Yes," Lafayette continued, bringing the speaking-trumpet back to his mouth, the attention of the soldiers gained. "Thundering, storm? Something... Storm Dog, Storm Mongrel, or was it Windy Something... Maybe Windy Pooch, Windy Mutt, or Breezy Bidge - no, maybe Pink Elephant... or something – you know these prairie-dog-types, it's so difficult to keep up with their naming conventions."

"If you are in collusion with this Savage, you'll be treated just as he is."

"Look at how he just stands there," the magician shook his head, "tempting *Fate...*"

Jacobi swore that Lafayette looked right at him through the binoculars for the briefest second.

"Reminds me of the time I once saw... *Thunder Hawk!* ...yes! That is his name, I knew it'd come back to me." Lafayette applied his showmanship. "Anyway, I once saw this particular prairie man stand up to a bear. It was roaring at him, growling, claws ready to rip him to shreds. The fool just stood there, locking eyes with the beast."

"Put the cone down! Is there a point to your incessant *yammering*?" Cordell's tolerance for civility had faded.

"There is. I implore your patience for just a moment longer. *So,* the bear didn't really calm down, but it did turn around and crawl away while having a raging fit. Thunder Hawk just stood there, as if he assumed the big ugly monster wouldn't kill him and would just lose interest and walk away."

Jacobi looked to Miller. "Did he... did... did Lafayette just tell me why Hawk is just standing there... with a story about a bear? Like, that the bear is Cordell and he'll just go away? Or that he won't go away like the bear?"

"Maybe, maybe not." Miller frowned. "But that bastard is using one of my stories. Lafayette never saw Hawk stand up to a bear – I did! *That's. My. Story.* I was there; not him. The fugging busdud!"

Twyla frowned. "I do indeed hope then that the bear story is not our sign...?"

Captain Cordell shook his knife before Lafayette's face, sensing that the man may actually possess knowledge beyond others.

"That's it. Both of you, kneel, hands behind your head."

"Fugg. We're too late," Miller stood up, ready to run in as Hawk and Lafayette obeyed.

Jacobi, before coming to the West, never would have trusted or believed in such a thing as Fate. He held the charm around his neck, waiting for a sign, somehow knowing, and raised a finger for his companions to, "Wait..."

"Fate has been kind," the Captain stated. "There will be two sacrifices today instead." The Captain looked about, as though he had a grander audience than those around him. "*Qonkura* will be pleased." Turning to the closest soldier, Cordell commanded, "Fetch the sacraments. We're doing this now."

"But Captain," Lafayette implored, "if you proceed with this course of action, you won't see that train we spoke of coming..."

Cordell frowned, turning back to his prisoners. "What train?"

The thing didn't have any of the comfortable familiarity that it should have.

A locomotive had come from the East toward Rubicon Crossing, impossibly, without making rumble, sight, or sound. From the smokestack, a plume of strangely cold green-white smoke followed it as transparent and ethereal as the cold vapour that shaped the volume of the engine and carriages that followed. It was a railroad terror usually reserved for horrific stories of the night - not the safe waking times of broad daylight.

The Captain looked up in time to see the ghost train arrive and pass through the magician's train car. His heart pumped with fright, as did his soldiers. The train should have smashed everything in its path apart, mashing bodies and splintering wood and steel, but the thing passed through them effortlessly.

Cordell caught sight of the train's driver - what appeared to be an ethereal apparition of Charles Lafayette with burning eyes. The spectre of the magician pointed into Cordell's soul as the phantom engine passed through him, emitting a deep guttural voice from depths unknown, *"Your train is on time, Captain..."*

"That's the sign - let's move!" Jacobi forced the binoculars back to Miller.

Around half the soldiers were panicked. Seeing a ghost train pass through their commanding officer and continue through the filed army, ignoring the physical need to stay on the railroad tracks, was certainly not an everyday comfortable military experience.

Nobody disagreed with Jacobi. Miller and Twyla both followed his sudden bold advance, the three all unsure of what just took place on the bridge, but welcomed it as their *sign*.

Some soldiers screamed to saviours that did not respond as others found that there was more comfort over the edge of the bridge, plummeting hundreds of feet to a river death rather than face the horror of the oncoming spectral engine.

They burst from their advantageous hiding place among the brush of a cliff edge, guns blazing, emboldened outlaws ready to rescue one of their own.

Those with the psychological mettle to withstand the terror of the oncoming apparition and those that were already more comfortable with such impossibilities, took up arms in response to the ghost train and subsequent ambush.

Hawk breathed with the relief that he was still alive after the phantom vehicle passed through him. It had knocked Cordell over with the sheer shock and unpreparedness of witnessing such an apparition before him.

"How?" Hawk asked, knowing all too well that there would be no answer forthcoming, "you were just... that train... Was that you on the train?"

"I'm sure I don't have the foggiest of ideas as to what you are rambling on about," Lafayette ignored the question, "but it's good to see you again, Old Friend. Oh, and I do sincerely apologise for referring to you as some sort of flea-ridden common mangy prairie dog - but you must understand the nature of conversing with these repugnant men?"

Hawk turned around, tapping a closed fist against his chest, smiling to the magician. "My thanks to you all the same."

Hawk and Lafayette darted behind the magician's caravan as rifle fire began finding its way near them over the fallen army captain.

"Take this." Lafayette handed him one of his matching decorated pistols - an exotic weapon by a revolver's standards - and some ammunition. "Did you know, that ruckus out there is a motley crew of desperados you assembled by rescuing a young man from this very river we rise above. He's leading them to your rescue. My word, how much that little boy from Boston has grown."

"It's now or never!" Jacobi shouted, raising a neckerchief over the lower half of his face. He charged toward the western end of Rubicon Crossing, revolvers bursting. Everything that had happened to Jacobi since falling from the paddle steamer into the Rubicon River had led to this.

Miller and Twyla flanked his either side, raising their own kerchief masks over their noses, shooting their rifles at opposing soldiers.

Jacobi realised, as did his allies, that Lafayette's special ammunition was something unexpected. "Hey, our bullets are on fire!" Sure enough, each round that found its mark didn't just pierce but also burst with a small firework of chromatic sparks that scorched and burned.

Buddy took off, barking, ahead of the three.

The panic among the soldiers flared as the ambush escalated. Opposing ammunition exploded with lights and caught aflame as their assailants appeared with the element of surprise. Many took cover between the wagons, although the army horses attached to them scrambled about frantically against what space remained on the bridge.

As soldiers closed in on the Indian and magician, Hawk and Lafayette returned fire with matching pistols.

Lafayette turned and ducked, only to return with his other outstretched white-gloved hand releasing decks of playing cards like springs from a novelty can. The cards fanned about the soldiers in a shower of gambled confusion.

In the moment of distraction, Hawk and Lafayette shot them with the same fiery effect as their friends at the other end of the bridge.

When the soldiers were dispatched, they realised that Cordell had ascended a wagon to uncover some sort of multi-barrelled machine gun. The horses attached to the wagon were limp with blood flowing from their throats, Cordell's peculiar knife still within one of them. Hawk saw the horses, slain by the captain simply so his weapon had a steady platform.

Hawk raised a pistol at Cordell, "You are without mercy," firing.

Captain Cordell ducked while turning the crank of the machine gun. The contraption sprang to life, spitting speeding ammunition ahead of itself. Rounds pounded and bit into the magician's caravan, splintering and cracking ancient wood. As alchemical parts of the caravan exploded inside, three shots found Lafayette.

The magician dropped his fancy pistol, blood gurgling upon his goatee and moustache. The machine gun rounds had speared through his body and into his wagon.

Hawk's fists curled and he sprang forward. Any last shred of forgiveness within his spirit that he had relearned when standing over a cowering Twyla Matthias faded. A bullet grazed his shoulder from a soldier, another from the machine gun, but he lunged toward the blue-uniformed Cordell with knuckles of vengeance.

Jacobi, Miller and Twyla had fought their way through the bridge but neared all too late. Buddy had mauled some soldiers, still rushing ahead.

Jacobi could hear the rise of a dread chorus; the clarion call of the Ghost Riders was nearing again. *Who was it for this time?* The weather was getting worse, storm clouds gathering at an unnatural pace, the two phenomena converging in unison.

"Human bodies are so frail..." Charles Lafayette backed onto the balustrade of the bridge, holding his chest as blood seeped through his fingers from his shirt and vest. "My train has come... When you speak of me... speak fondly..."

Cordell's crank still turned, trying to mow down the Indian and the magician with a weapon created for attacking across a field of battle. Machine gun rounds found the caravan again and more esoteric things inside detonated.

The magician's caravan erupted in a ball of coloured fiery lightning. As the hissed squeal of a cat painfully pierced all minds nearby, the blast of firework-like energy smashed Lafayette over the edge of the bridge to plunge hundreds of yards into the rushing Rubicon River below.

Charles Lafayette's mystery washed away with the plummeting impact and the power of the raging waters flowing from waterfalls to the north.

"No!" Miller ducked behind a wagon, reloading, then firing at whoever fired at him. He may not have enjoyed the magician's company, but he didn't need to see him blasted away like that. Twyla took a bullet to the chest, forced to take cover with Miller. The whole scene felt like reliving the Civil War. "Fugginell, Woman, I'm not losing you too!"

"Hawk!" Jacobi almost reached him, forcing Cordell from their fistfight with some frenzied revolver fire. He only had a second to reflect upon Lafayette's demise among the chaos before revealing the Indian's tomahawk, throwing the weapon to its owner.

It was caught. Hawk spun with the weapon, using the flat of the blade to drop the Captain. He then held with the axe-edge over Cordell's skull. Hawk was ready to kill the relentless butcher once and for all.

As he contemplated the events around his spiritually significant tool, time seemed to slow, and his life replayed before his eyes as thunder cracked overhead.

The weather had shifted severely in an instant. Grey clouds had collected, creating what seemed like the onset of an irregular night sky forcing away the day. Over Rubicon Crossing they fell rolling forth like a heavy fog from a broken sky.

The Ghost Riders...

Jacobi shouted as rain fell across the area. "Surely you're seeing them this time?" As the former Bostonian turned away, the scars on his face from the Terror Gator glowed like the embers of mythical brimstone, the scars of his body trying to shine through his western clothing. Jacobi gave Hawk ballistic cover, revolver with firework rounds in hand.

Hawk was seeing them. At last, he was seeing them. He was seeing all of it. All of *them*. He was finally witnessing the Ghost Riders. "I do..." He looked at the charm of *Fate*, the Aetron, hanging around Jacobi's neck. "Thanks to you, I finally do."

"It's not me..." Jacobi understood something, something intangible - seeing it, sensing it – almost as though the ineffable Web

of Fate could actually be tangible. "It's you...
You closed yourself off to everything, you cut
yourself away from the threads of *Fate* before
they could warn you about the path you were
going to travel. They've always been with you,
trying to reach you, but others have needed to
see them for you. Until now... Everything has
changed. It's all connected."

Buddy pounced at a soldier, growling with
dripping fangs, his fur like spines of fire, eyes
like glowing coals. He tore shreds of flesh and
blue uniform, soldiers screaming of a
"Hellhound!" The dog pounced about the bridge
with a preternatural agility appearing as a beast
from Below.

A bullet knocked Twyla's bonnet off while
another found its purchase in her chest again.
Instead of screaming with pain, the tomahawk
scar upon her usually porcelain scalp spewed
with a hot red light from a place nobody dared to
know. She pulled Miller up from their place of
cover, the two emboldened by the meteorological
arrival of the Ghost Riders, to unleash a torrent
of exploding ammunition back upon their
attacking soldiers.

Miller sprang away, having a group of
soldiers on the run westward along the bridge.
The veteran's coat burned with fire, transforming
it grey. Another fire reformed the coat to blue. A
third fire returned his coat to that of the outlaw

he had become. His eyes burned with the raging fires of war, his entire body smouldering with a smoke from Beyond.

As Hawk held Cordell, pinned under the tomahawk upon his skull, the Indian heard a wave of rolling thunder followed by the unrelenting cracking of a storm. A giant bird, the likes of which he hadn't seen in his visions for years, swooped with a group of the Ghost Riders from the East flying West. The colossal bird shook its massive head, lightning shooting from its eyes into the Indian. Chortling with the sound of a thunderstorm, it flew straight into Hawk's chest, disappearing with a snap-hiss of sparks.

Jacobi needed to know. "You saw that, right, that giant bird just flew to you... with the others out there, you can still see all this, right?"

"I do." Hawk smiled to Jacobi, his eyes swirling with snapping sparks. "And I see *Jacobi-Nicholson-no-more,* instead an *Outlaw of the West*, you whom *Fate* weaved into this, leading us all to the here-and-now, in defiance of those who do not respect the West."

Just as his soldiers were, Captain Cordell was also witnessing the terrifying apparitions. "Get off me! What is this?" Despite a familiarity to such unnatural things, fear still gripped the wounded army captain. Fear, and outrage at the defiance of these criminals.

"You'll be executed as an outlaw if you don't shoot this savage off me now!" Cordell still tried to free himself while barking at Jacobi. "Who do you think you are, helping this prairie dog?"

Jacobi studied the necklace Hawk had given him when they first met: the whittled wood fashioned like a mix between a snowflake and a spider's web... "Good question." Jacobi knew who he was and what he had become in this Wild West, giving Cordell the answer that *Fate* had led him to.

"I am Jac... I'm *Jake...* Jake the Outlaw..." He raised his arms to draw attention to the spirits swirling about the bridge. "And we... we are the *Ghost Riders!*"

Hawk felt a unifying sensation from the thunder that followed Jacobi's words - from this new *Jake.* These spectral beings had presented a moral choice each time they appeared to an individual, but this time those past witnesses had become their metaphysical extensions.

"And I..." the Indian looked to Jake, knowing that he knew of the stories, "I am *Thunder Hawk,* Spiritwalker of the Wakoda."

Thunder Hawk's face became a skull, his long hair waves of fire. "The Ghost Riders," he waved his tomahawk around at the immaterial riders and their living counterparts, "will decide your Fate."

To stop him escaping, Thunder Hawk sunk his tomahawk blade into Cordell's leg rather than his head. As the soldier screamed, the Indian used the same ropes that had bound him during his forced march from Sundown to tie him to the balustrade of Rubicon Crossing where Lafayette had fallen.

After losing more soldiers, morale was low among the army. Those that could, fled their leader. Jake Nicholson, Alfred Miller, Twyla Matthias and Buddy came before Thunder Hawk and a tethered Cordell while continuing to return fire upon any remaining soldiers. Their terrifying veneers mocked him. Each one had the means - and some the motive - to kill the Captain and it tore apart his ego that he was at their mercy.

"Betrayer." He recognised Twyla. "How could you have fallen in with such a lot? We would have had everything. *Qonkura* rewards those who conquer."

She didn't know who or what clandestine thing he referred to. She nodded to Jacobi, "I would rather fall in with this *posse* than continue to fall as far as you have."

Cordell faced Jacobi. "Beware of the path you are walking, *Jake the Outlaw*." The Captain's stare bore right into his soul. "Heed my warning and turn back now; *follow no dreams*."

Despite her wounds, Twyla punched Cordell across the face, knocking their enemy unconscious. "Now that's how you hit somebody properly," she explained to Miller.

Jake whooped while wondering what Cordell's mysterious words meant as Twyla shook her aching fist. The spectral riders surrounding began to fade away, as did the hellish guises of the outlaws.

Reunited with the husky as his usual red and white furred self, Buddy became the focus of many warm greetings.

"Fugg!" Miller was looking north-east through his binoculars. "Reinforcements from Fort Morgan are riding in fast. They were probably wondering where Cordell and his prisoner are. We gotta go. I doubt we'll get a second chance-

"We need to search for Lafayette's body," Twyla interrupted, waving at the charred remains of the magician's caravan.

"Chuck's gone." Miller had to hide the water in his eyes. "Nobody drops from Rubicon Crossing and lives to tell about it. He's 'gator bait now."

It was difficult to accept for all of them, but Charles Lafayette was gone – and they all heard the dying feline hiss of his cat, Memphis, in their minds.

Jake called, firing at some remaining soldiers. "Alright then, we've got Thunder Hawk, let's get out of here!"

"We'll need to hide for a while until all this passes," Thunder Hawk stated. "Cordell can wake up to the Fate of his own moral compass, as we've all had to do in the past. "I'm sorry that my need for vengeance brought you all into this mess, but we may as well stay together for now."

"Twyla put it well before," Jake added.

"Put what well?" Miller's brow raised.

"We're a *posse*... that's what we've become."

"Yep." Miller dropped the binoculars around his neck. "I'll ride with this posse."

They hadn't realised it until this moment, but that's exactly what they had become: a posse.

As the outlaws fought their way from Rubicon Crossing to their horses, Thunder Hawk caught sight of a familiar black domestic cat prancing casually over a rocky outcropping. "Is that...?"

The cat paused, regally, noting the posse, then disappeared into the brush.

"Is that, what?" Miller asked.

"Nothing..." Thunder Hawk smiled to himself. "It'd only annoy you."

"Are you all mysterious again now?" Miller laughed. "People, Thunder Hawk has returned!"

They would ride together with haste out of there, Buddy running faithfully alongside. The constant threat of the pursuing army would be like lighting striking behind them. They were going to ride faster and further than any of them had ever rode before.

Jake pointed as far West as possible into the setting sun. "Okay, *posse*, let's ride!"

He accepted that Fate had bound them together in ways he was only beginning to understand. They were outlaws of the West now, a nameless posse...

Or were they?

EPILOGUE

BOUND BY FATE

"Let the Lady go..."

It was almost midnight. Elizabeth would never dream of roaming Sundown after dark unless it was absolutely necessary. She needed to find which saloon her Father was in as one of their horses was about to give birth. She'd managed to politely avoid the many grubby hands in Sundowner Saloon and was moving on to try at the Pig and Swig, but the persistent reaching of one man had followed her despite her many refusals.

The shadowy visage took the pursuer and the pursued by surprise, suddenly appearing ahead of them in an alleyway full of piled crates that Elizabeth had attempted to lose the man through. Under the poor starlight, the tilted brim of a hat hid most of the shadowy visage's features. Only a scarred jaw of stubble revealed the mouth that had given the command. Its hands were loose, jacket slightly revealing a holstered revolver.

"Get out of here, Mister," the pursuer slurred, "she's with me."

"No, I'm not." Elizabeth used the moment to move away. "I'm not with this man. I'm trying to find my Father."

"Francis Geddes..." The shadowy visage knew the name of the woman's pursuer, its breath a ghostly white against the cold night. "Let the Lady go or be damned to ride for eternity among us."

Francis had drunk too much. Again.

Despite a stroke of good luck that had freed him from the servitude of the mines of Boom Town, his personality was always his own worst enemy. It was only a matter of time before his incessant voice and actions landed him in another hazardous situation such as this.

"No, she's mine!" Francis stumbled, trying to put on a gruff exterior. "And how do you know my name?"

An arrow shot from behind the shadowy visage, piercing Francis by his shirt to a stacked wooden crate.

Elizabeth didn't know what to do. "Thank you, thank you, Mister. I'll go now. I'll go." She counted her blessings and headed back out of the alley, heading home instead of chancing another Sundown night encounter. Damn her Father, she decided to take care of the birth herself.

"Francis Geddes," the shadowy visage said again, tossing a leather pouch. "Return to the East, leave the West; or ride with us forevermore."

The bag clinked as it landed at Francis' feet. It sounded hefty, full of coins. "With us? How do you know...? There's only you. Who are you?"

A lantern came to life as Francis tore his shirt to lean down for the bag, freeing himself.

A group had been waiting silently in the night. A dark brown horse with white blaze stood riderless behind the shadowy visage. Further behind, a weathered man with greying beard held the lantern atop a grey horse. A woman bearing a deep scar across her forehead sat side-saddle upon a brown and white steed. Another man with long black hair held an antler bow aimed with an arrow upon a golden-tan horse with tiger stripes. A red husky with peculiar eyes groaned with ill will toward Francis while a black cat crossed between him and the shadowy visage.

Jake - the shadowy visage - tipped his hat, Francis fleeing into the night toward the train station from the answer.

"We are the Ghost Riders."

BROKEN WINGS

Erica's father wasn't aware of the terrifying monster that lurked below their ranch in the abandoned gold mine.

If he had known, he may not have announced that he was going to build a Flying Machine by the Fourth of July. He may not have worked on the contraption with such a manic fever, oblivious of his dying wife. And, he may have been able to avoid the monster feeding on what was left of his fragile mind.

For Erica's father, the Flying Machine and his quest for the sky had to succeed - nothing else mattered!

SPOILER ALERT!

THERE'S AN EXTRACT OVER THE PAGE.

WYRD WEST

BROKEN WINGS

L.T. PHOENIX

Broken Wings

Copyright © L.T. Phoenix 2021

Published by Phoenix Forge.

Print: ISBN: 9780994642646
Digital ISBN: 9780994642622

2.2

BROKEN WINGS

"His nearness to the devouring sun softened the fragrant wax that held the wings: and the wax melted: he flailed with bare arms, but losing his oar-like wings, could not ride the air. Even as his mouth was crying his father's name, it vanished into the dark blue sea, the Icarian Sea, called after him."

– Ovid
"Metamorphoses,
Bk VIII:183-235 Daedalus and Icarus"

FOREWORD

What follows are the journal entries of patient Erica Voland as she recounts the alleged events that led to her father's apparent descent into madness, including a manic quest to build a flying machine and the discovery of a terrifying monster that dwelled in an abandoned gold mine below their ranch.

Collated by Doctor Perry Berkshire
Columbia Asylum for the Mentally Insane
La Grande, Wakoda Territory

FIRST ENTRY

"My Flying Machine will soar from the ranch by the Fourth of July!" Papa had claimed at the supper table. "And, Erica," he pointed at me, "you'll be writing everything down as I go."

Mama coughed from behind her kerchief, straining to speak. "Don't forget about the ranch." While her condition was getting worse, she still knew she had to rein Papa in whenever he had yet another idea for another crazy scheme.

"Don't worry," Papa assured, "by writing down everything about the Flying Machine, Erica's book-skills can finally be used for something useful."

"Papa..." I frowned.

"Well, you've already scared away anyone in the area that'd make a good husband by showing you can read and talk back smart. You're nineteen now, you shouldn't have your nose in books... You should be learning to be like your Mama in the kitchen."

I tried not to let my blood boil.

"You'll put it in a useful book, maybe we'll try to get one of them photographs of it, sell the Flying Machine book, make more money than the ranch has ever seen. We could sell the ranch, pack up, and with all the money we could move to La Grande and find a real nice place, find a good doctor that'll fix Mama up real nice too... You'll see."

Our property, branded by the rusting sign at the front gate as *Matthias Ranch*, had been bought years ago from the woman known across the territory as the *Gold Baroness*. Papa always says he, "Bought it for a steal." It was an opportunity too good to pass on for settlers wanting to start ranching in the West. He and Mama didn't have much to begin with and this Twyla Matthias lady was willing to part with her ranch for far less than Papa valued it at.

All on account of her husband being killed by Indians while working the ranch...

Papa just assumed that the Gold Baroness wanted to move on, leave the bad memory behind, so she didn't care for how much. Even without any livestock included, the ranch had been bought cheap.

And Papa always said, time and again, that if the Indians were going to be a problem for the ranch that he'd simply just keep all his rifles loaded in case of any hostility from them.

SECOND ENTRY

During one supper, a few days later, there came a terrifying shriek from outside the house.

It was the kind of screech that pumps your blood so much that you think you will jump out of your skin. It was piercing - so sharp, as though the sound stabbed right through your ears and into to your skull.

"Wolves?" Mama coughed.

Papa was already to a rifle leaning near the fireplace and took a lantern from the mantle. "I dunno. Don't sound like any wolves I ever heard. Maybe something new – maybe whatever got the dog..."

Despite the loss of our dog being a sore spot for us all, Papa burst out the door with the lantern already lit, holding it aloft, trying to see what was happening.

Mama and I drew closer to the doorway, seeing something scurry past - except, it *was* there and it *wasn't* there.

As Papa put the lantern down on the porch so he could take his rifle in two hands, we noticed the arrows on the dirt just before the first step of the porch.

They were Indian arrows. Three of them.

Papa waved his gun about in our small area of lit darkness. "Who goes there?" He wasn't really asking for anybody; it was more of a demand of the night to alleviate the feeling of the unknown.

Somebody was out there, though.

They lit a torch, throwing the flaming brand between us all on the bare dirt, expanding the sphere of light available in the unquiet night.

It was an Indian – no mistake! – sitting atop a well-packed horse that had striped legs.

"A friend," he responded in our language, and quite well, to Papa's question that hadn't really been a question.

Papa levelled his rifle at the Indian. "The last time you lot was here, you killed the man of the ranch. That's not going to happen again. Get the fugg out of here now."

The Indian slowly placed what must have been the bow that shot the arrows upon his horse's neck. It was an odd weapon, seemingly composed of antlers. As he held his hands up to

signal surrender, we really got our best look at
him.

His long hair fell about a bare chest that
was painted with some sort of mural in red;
three vertical strokes crossing three horizontal
strokes set among three circular strokes, all
evenly spaced.

Why this particular detail resonated in my
mind so profoundly over any other painted
marks and native decorations, I don't know, but
the Indian's mural had some form of frightening
beauty to it.

"I am not of the ones responsible," the
Indian answered, commanding a noble
countenance, "just as you are not responsible for
deaths among my people when this was our
land."

"No, but I don't care. I bought this land fair,
even have *Uncle Sam's* papers."

Papa was taking aim. I had seen it many
times before when he was shooting on the
property.

Then the Indian said the strangest thing. "I
have been tracking a monster over this land. It
has been targeting your ranch to feed."

"*Monster?* Well, I can handle the wild
animals, Indian. Nothing but some foxes and
occasional wolves to worry about." He put more
emphasis on aiming the rifle, ignoring the fact
that something strange had killed our dog

recently. "I'm going to give you to the count of three."

The Indian pointed to the arrows on the ground just near our porch steps. "This is no wild animal. Do you see blood?"

Papa was trying to be careful of any tricks, but he could also see what Mama and I could see. The crude arrow heads were splashed with silver, leaving small pools of the shining liquid on the dirt.

"Indian poison," Papa explained, convincing himself that he wasn't going to be fooled by any native nonsense.

"It is what flows through the monster. It has fled for what remains of its life into the cave on your property."

"The abandoned mine?" Papa frowned.

I had never seen an Indian up close, but I'm sure this native man was being as sincere as he could be while having a gun pointed at his head.

"If I could track it further into-

Papa fired the rifle; a warning shot inches from the Indian's hair. "Get off my land, and if I see you anywhere inside the fences of my property again... I'll shoot to kill! You and any other savages you got with you out there."

The Indian tracker steadied his bow and took his reigns, carefully, and directed his horse away. When he was almost out of the sphere of

light, he looked back directly at Mama and said,
"I am sorry, I have done all I can..."

GHOST RIDERS

The Civil War is over. American expansion pushes westward across the United States, unaware of the supernatural dangers that lurk in the Wild West.

A Bostonian tourist is thrust against his will into this savage land of outlaws and desperados. Finding allies in a war veteran, a native tracker, a gold rush baroness, a mysterious magician and a trusty dog, Jacobi Nicholson will find that he is destined to heal some of the scars this unforgiving landscape has given his new friends.

Bound by the spectres of an old frontier myth, will the gang defy the Law to do what is right and go beyond legend...?

DREAD RECKONING

Royce Falco is scheduled for execution in the Hayworth Penitentiary.

His usual confidence to slip from such situations is crushed when a mysterious visitor brings news that his demise has been orchestrated, but also brings an offer to alter his fate... the decision will come at a price.

Dread sets in as Royce's last midnight approaches in the reputably haunted prison, because at 5 o'clock they take him to the gallows post.

HORSE NATION

Matteo and Nickolas Tobin have spent years using their career as surveyors to fund their side project of investigating supernatural phenomena across the Wild West.

A native Wakoda ritual that the brothers stumble upon while exploring the area of Otter Creek will change them forever when they discover that the forces of Fate had destined them to be participants in the ceremony.

Whether Matteo and Nickolas will accept their role in that destiny is another matter.

SILENT ECHOES

An entire train and its passengers have mysteriously vanished from Echo Station overnight without a trace.

The only clues to solving the impossible occurence arrive in the form of a series of increasingly frantic messages that were telegraphed to the town of Sundown during the night of the vanishing. Descriptions abound of sinister men in beaked masks and heavy cloaks that the sender names as plague doctors, and monsters that remain unnamed.

With only the raving telegraphs as evidence, this may be an investigation that can't be solved.